"Bring Yourself in a Sack" Mrs. Shepard called this project when she assigned it last Friday as part of our unit on creative writing. There was a brown paper lunch bag on each desk when we got to class after lunch. Mrs. Shepard said, "Fill the bag with ten items that represent you in all your many aspects." Maybe she said facets. Either way, I thought it sounded like a cool project.

Anyway.

I'm lying low in my seat, now, clutching the bag and squeezing my eyes shut as Mrs. Shepard speaks. "I want to hear a clear, concise explanation of each item, why you chose it, and what, about your character, the item symbolizes."

We have to explain? I would've chosen all different things.

I don't know what I was thinking would happen with this Sack. Definitely NOT that I would have to unload my life from this brown paper bag like spreading my lunch on the cafeteria table for everybody to inspect and judge. No, no. Thanks anyway.

OTHER BOOKS YOU MAY ENJOY

Not That I Care

THE FRIENDSHIP RING

rachel vail

Four rings. One promise:
Best Friends Forever

Not That I Care

PUFFIN BOOKS
An Imprint of Penguin Group (USA)

PUFFIN BOOKS
Published by the Penguin Group
Penguin Group (USA) LLC
375 Hudson Street
New York, New York 10014

USA * Canada * UK * Ireland * Australia
New Zealand * India * South Africa * China

penguin.com
A Penguin Random House Company

First published in the United States of America by Scholastic Inc., 1998
Published by Puffin Books, an imprint of Penguin Young Readers Group, 2014

Library of Congress Cataloging-in-Publication Data is available.

Puffin Books ISBN 978-0-14-751120-1

Printed in the United States of America

1 3 5 7 9 10 8 6 4 2

to Ronnie and Ed,

in anticipation of future celebrations

Not That I Care

one

No way. I didn't know we were going to have to stand up in front of the entire class. There's no sound in the classroom except the *click, click* of Mrs. Shepard's pointy pumps on the tile floor. She's behind me now, so I can't see her. She hasn't even said hello. Creative writing and American history are too important, I guess, and we are too shockingly ignorant to waste a second. Mrs. Shepard seems insulted that our sixth-grade teacher thought we were ready for her class.

"When I call your name," she says, "please bring your Sack to the front of the room and stand beside my desk."

I don't know what to look at. This is a new thing

with me. Lately my face has trouble knowing what to do. I catch myself blinking too hard, or chewing my upper lip, or with my mouth hanging open. My face can't relax, like it used to. It doesn't quite fit me anymore.

I blow my bangs off my eyelashes and try to sit still. *Count to five without moving*, my mother keeps telling me, *I can't stand how fidgety you are lately, Morgan*. One, two, three, I can't do it. I have to shift my shoulders around.

"Bring Yourself in a Sack" Mrs. Shepard called this project when she assigned it last Friday as part of our unit on creative writing. There was a brown paper lunch bag on each desk when we got to class after lunch. Mrs. Shepard said, "Fill the bag with ten items that represent you in all your many aspects." Maybe she said facets. Either way, I thought it sounded like a cool project.

Lou Hochstetter, who sits behind me, had complained that we don't usually get homework over the weekend. Mrs. Shepard raised one eyebrow and stared at poor Lou for a mini-eternity, until he sunk down so low his feet clanged my chair's legs. "Welcome to the seventh grade, Mr. Hochstetter," she said. That cracked me up.

After school, my best friend, CJ Hurley, got asked out. She called me right away to tell me, of course, but I was out riding my bike around. Friday had been a stressful day, socially. CJ left me a message on the machine: "Hello, this is a message for Morgan— Morgan? Tommy Levit just asked me out. Call me." All weekend I kept meaning to call her back, but I just didn't get a chance. Not that I wasn't happy for her. I don't like Tommy anymore.

I just really got into this project, searching for ten perfect things. I barely talked to anybody. "Bring Yourself in a Sack?" my brother asked. "I remember that project." But I didn't want his help.

I was in a great mood when I got to school this morning, with my Sack full of ten complicated, meaningful symbols. The janitor was just unlocking the front doors, I got to school so early. I slid my bike into the rack and waited on the wall for CJ.

When her mother dropped her off, CJ ran over and climbed up onto the wall beside me. She didn't say anything about my not calling her back; she knows I'm really bad about that and she's used to it. Or I thought so, anyway. We talked about Tommy. I told her not to worry that they didn't talk all weekend, after the asking out; when I went out with him last year he never called me, either. Then we talked about whether Tommy's twin brother, Jonas, would ask me out today, like he was supposed to, and how fun it would be if the four of us were a foursome, and whether or not Jonas's curly hair is goofy. CJ used to like Jonas, but now she's going out with Tommy, which is fine with me.

Not that she cares.

I guess actually, now that I think about it, I was doing all the chatting. CJ wasn't saying anything about becoming a foursome. She was just sitting there all pale, her deep-set green eyes looking anywhere but at me, her tight, skinny body even tauter than usual. I didn't notice she was acting weird until too late.

Anyway.

Mrs. Shepard is walking up toward the front of the class. I hold my breath while she passes me. When my brother, Ned, was in seventh grade, four years ago, he said Mrs. Shepard was "real" because she wouldn't paste stars on every pretentious, childish poem full of clichés. I took my poem off the refrigerator. I vowed I'd make Mrs. Shepard like me when I got to seventh grade. So far she doesn't, particularly, but it's only the third week of school. I still have a shot.

I'm lying low in my seat now, clutching the bag and squeezing my eyes shut as Mrs. Shepard speaks. "I want to hear a clear, concise explanation of each item, why you chose it, and what about your character the item symbolizes."

We have to explain? I would've chosen all different things.

I don't know what I was thinking would happen with this Sack. Definitely NOT that I would have to unload my life from this brown paper bag like spreading my lunch on the cafeteria table for everybody to inspect and judge. No, no. Thanks anyway.

"Are there any questions?" Mrs. Shepard asks.

Right. Nobody raises a hand with a question, of course. I can't look around to see if everybody else seems relaxed and ready, if it's just me who's hiding under a desk.

"Good," Mrs. Shepard says, turning her helmet-head to look at each of us. Her white-blond hair is pasted into the kind of hairdo that never moves, the kind that only gets washed once a week, at the beauty parlor. She reminds me of an owl, with her round, piercing eyes and small hooked nose. Maybe it's the way she rotates her big head that's plunked deep between her shoulders. I did a report last year on owls. They're birds of prey. I sink down lower, imagining myself a field mouse trying to camouflage with the fake wood and putty-colored metal of my desk.

Please don't call on me.

"Olivia Pogostin," Mrs. Shepard calls.

Olivia Pogostin is my new best friend, as of today. I whispered with her all through lunch, which was a little awkward for both of us, but we managed. She was actually sort of witty, and she gets the pretzel sticks that come in an individually wrapped box in her lunch, definitely a plus. My mother would never waste the money on those. We buy economy-size everything, then take how much we need. We have one type of cookies for weeks at a time, until we finish and go back to Price Club. If there's a big sale, she might let us get a sleeve of individual potato chip bags. I always feel good if I open my lunch and there's a small sealed bag of chips in there. It looks so appropriate. CJ just gets a yogurt, every day, a yogurt, and that's it. Not that they can't afford more. She just has to worry, because of ballet.

I sort of liked Olivia today at lunch. Not as deadly wonkish as I had always figured. She had some funny things to say about girls like CJ who forget their friends as soon as a boy calls her on the phone. And, of course, there's the pretzels.

Olivia walks up to the front of the class. Her coarse black pigtails don't bounce, just jut adamantly out to the sides. She's the smallest person in seventh grade by a lot, and also the smartest if you don't count Ken Carpenter.

Olivia places her brown paper bag on Mrs. Shepard's desk, turns to face the class, and says in her calm, steady monotone, "So. This is me."

What am I going to do? I can't present my items.

My palms are starting to sweat on the brown paper of my Sack. This is me? No way I would ever get up and say This is me. Especially with this unexplainable stuff to explain.

Olivia pulls a charcoal pencil out of her paper bag, holds it up in front of her serious face, and announces, "Charcoal pencils, because I like to draw." She places it on Mrs. Shepard's desk blotter. Mrs. Shepard is nodding, over by the door. Teachers love Olivia; she does everything right. I didn't know it was supposed to be like hobbies.

"A calculator," Olivia says, lifting it. Her eyes focus above our heads on the back wall. "Because math is my favorite subject." She sets it down.

I catch myself twirling the bottom of my black polo shirt and force myself to stop. My eyes, betraying me, glance over to my left. Next to me, CJ is sitting straight as a two-by-four on the edge of her chair, her head balanced gracefully on her long neck.

Olivia reaches into her Sack and pulls out a small box. I clamp my jaw shut and count. Sit up straight. My posture is just as good as CJ's.

Olivia pulls a pair of earrings out of the box. I can't stop blinking.

"These are soccer ball earrings, which represent me both because soccer is my favorite sport and also because I just got my ears pierced this summer."

Olivia glances at Mrs. Shepard, who hasn't budged. Ned told me that one time Mrs. Shepard told him, "Well said," and the whole class practically fainted.

Olivia swallows hard. Poor Olivia. I wonder what she's thinking. I don't know her that well, yet, but I'm sure she's off balance, not having the teacher nodding at her for once. If Olivia looks at me, I decide, I'll smile encouragingly. It must be hard, sort of, to expect praise all the time. Not that I'd know; I'm just guessing.

I prepare to be supportive. Olivia doesn't look at me. Which is fine. Whatever. She doesn't look at anybody else, either, at least. Staring at the back wall, she pulls a thick paperback book out of her bag. "A dictionary, because I'm interested in etymology," she says.

I have no idea what that means. Nothing in my bag can be explained in a sentence. I did the whole thing wrong. What am I going to do?

"A pool ball, because I like to shoot pool."

Oh, shut up already, Olivia, I almost say out loud. I open my crumpled brown bag just enough to peek inside. Wrong, wrong, wrong; no pool balls, no charcoal pencils. I have a broken thermometer. A Barbie head. A twig. Nothing I could possibly explain to these nineteen other seventh graders who've known me my whole life but have no clue. Not even CJ has a clue what's in here, and I am not at all interested in confessing. Not even to CJ who was my best friend from the beginning of fourth grade until today.

I'm twirling the bottom of my shirt with my finger again. It shames me if my clothes are wrinkled, it looks like I'm poor. Stop it. Pay attention to Olivia. My best friend. I blow the long bangs out of my eyes. They drive me crazy, but at least they hide the pimples on my forehead, four of them and a fresh one coming. Don't touch, the oil from fingers makes it worse. Think, think—what am I going to do? The backs of my thighs are sticking to the chair. Olivia is finishing, thank the Lord. I don't know if we're supposed to clap or what. I'm not going to be the first one. I wedge my hands under my thighs and blow at my bangs again.

I don't know what I was thinking. It's not like I'm so close with Mrs. Shepard I want her to be in on all my private business; in fact, I don't really like her at all, the owl. I just got so involved, all weekend, choosing my ten items, I didn't think of how they'd be presented. I guess I thought we'd just hand our Sacks in.

Olivia is heading back to her seat, the desk in front of mine. I make the mistake of glancing toward CJ again. She looks at me with a big sad apology all over her face.

Save it, pal. It's not like I care or anything. I'm just

trying to get through the day, and please, you are totally free to do whatever you want. It makes no difference, I've dealt with more than you'll ever know, you pampered little prima donna. It would take a lot more than you to hurt me.

two

Before my father left, we were a happy family. Or at least I think we were; I remember us always smiling and having lots of birthday parties. Actually, maybe I only remember what's in the photo albums.

Maybe we weren't that happy. I don't know. I guess we were normal.

My parents were hoping for a girl when Mom was pregnant with me. On the way to the hospital, the day I was born, my mother saw a cherry tree in someone's yard, all the cherries hanging down like ornaments, like jewelry, and she made my father promise that if she delivered a girl, he'd plant her a cherry tree like the one in that yard.

Shockingly enough, my father did as he promised, and when Mom came home from the hospital with me all in pink, Dad yanked us out back to see. Four-year-old Ned was standing out there all covered in dirt, proudly showing me and Mom the little sapling cherry tree he and my dad had planted. Mom cried. She used to cry pretty easily.

They took a picture of me lying on a baby blanket in front of the little tree. I was three days old, and I look like a wise but cranky little old man. They used the picture for my birth announcement. We proudly introduce our daughter, Morgan Amanda Miller . . .

Every year on my birthday, Dad used to sit me in front of the cherry tree in jeans and a white shirt and take a picture. We have them arranged in a special book, like time-lapse photography: me holding my toes at one, me cute and spunky with bobbed hair when I was five, me with a missing-tooth-space in my mouth when I was turning eight, long, dark hair covering most of my face on my tenth, right before Mom chopped bangs on me. And behind me in each picture, the tree grew bigger and flowered, until there was a lacy spread of pinkish-white branches behind me by the time I was six—but no cherries, not a single cherry hung down off those branches like a piece of gaudy jewelry, even as the tree towered above me.

It became sort of a family joke, the cherry tree that grew no cherries.

I was best friends back then with a girl named Roxanne Luse, because she lives down the street and she's my age. Roxanne made up silly words for everything from passing gas (*gweezing*) and what's in your nose (*galloochi*) to ponytail holders (*zapoos*). She lost her first tooth in kindergarten and described to me in detail her late-night conversations with the tooth fairy, who paid her a crisp dollar for each tooth that fell out. No matter how much I wiggled my teeth and how much sugar I ate, everything in my mouth was anchored tight. My mother, annoyingly, told me my teeth were just healthy and strong.

Roxanne was very sympathetic. She told me she'd mentioned my name to TF, as she called the tooth fairy, and that TF had told her some people are just slow and that's fine. I felt grossly babyish. Roxanne looked so much more grown up, even at six, with all those spaces in her mouth and that wild mess of hair she refused to brush. She outweighed me by half.

Roxanne invented complicated imaginative games with endless rules I could never remember, because there were always new ones. Our favorite game was Time Machine, which we played under my cherry tree. Roxanne was the pilot of our time shuttle (called a *maznoropa*), so she got to say where we'd go— Colonial America, a prehistoric cave, Jupiter. Whatever the time period, she played my slave, and she told me exactly what I had to do. Then she'd make daring escapes or else die tragically. It was all a little scary to me, but there were no other kids my age around, and Ned was already too cool to let me play with him in the daytime.

Roxanne decided she should be called Rock, because of her name, and I should be called Tree, because of my cherry tree, which I had told her I owned. The tree evened things out in my mind: She got to make all the rules, but I owned something huge, living, and unmovable.

Roxanne swore we were part Native American, a fact provable because who else would have names like Rock and Tree? She also decided we were half cousins. I wasn't sure how we could prove that, but I didn't press. She said if the tree ever grew some cherries I could change my name to Cherry. I was psyched; Cherry seemed like a really beautiful name. Each time before we played Time Machine we'd check all the branches really carefully, and Roxanne would sympathetically announce, "No, your name is still Tree." Then I'd crouch down in my passenger spot and wait to see what time period the *maznoropa* would bring us to.

three

"Roxanne Luse," Mrs. Shepard says.

I look behind me to the right toward Roxanne. Her face is hidden in her hands, under her big tangle of black hair. Her green pants have writing all over them, and her T-shirt is on backward so the pocket is over her shoulder blade. She's not answering. *Come on, Rock*, I think, though I never call her that anymore. I know she would have interesting stuff in her bag; weird, even.

"Roxanne Luse," Mrs. Shepard says again.

"Unprepared," Roxanne mumbles into her hands.

"Unprepared?" Mrs. Shepard asks, like the word tastes sour in her mouth.

Roxanne lifts her head and stares at Mrs. Shepard.

"Unprepared?" Mrs. Shepard asks again.

"Yeah," Roxanne says and shrugs.

"That's unacceptable," says Mrs. Shepard.

Roxanne uncaps a Sharpie marker and starts to write on her pants.

"Gather your things," Mrs. Shepard says, looking at her watch. "Go to the office."

Roxanne fills in the shape she's drawn, recaps the Sharpie, and throws it into her big book bag. She pulls the book bag up onto her lap and sweeps the notebook, pens, and crumpled paper off her desk, into the bag, then smooshes it down with the heel of her hand. Then she sighs and stands up, hoisting the big bag onto her shoulder. Down the aisle she trudges and out the door.

Mrs. Shepard closes it quietly but firmly behind her and looks suspiciously at the rest of us. "Is anyone else here unprepared?"

Nobody moves or even breathes. She waits. The clock ticks. I consider raising my hand for one demented second, picture myself gathering my things and running down the hall to meet Rock and maybe be best friends with her again, no matter how weird and unpopular she is; at least it would get me out of having to stand up there in front, soon, and present this Sack full of myself.

I don't, of course. I sit very still.

"Let's continue," Mrs. Shepard says.

four

In the winter of second grade I started taking ballet after school on Tuesdays. It was sort of boring, but I liked having a chance to do something apart from Roxanne and her complicated games. She'd wait for me in her green Snorkel and boots under my cherry tree on Tuesdays, but sometimes I'd tell her I had to go inside and practice ballet, so she should go home. The ballet teacher told my mother after class one day that she should really encourage my ballet training because I was blessed with perfect turn-out. I ran to the backyard to show Roxanne, who said she had a headache and couldn't stay. At dinner Mom told Dad and Ned.

"Perfect turn-out?" asked Dad. "I'm ever so proud."

They all laughed, which humiliated me. I ran to

my room and slammed the door. I could hear them laughing straight through it. Our house is very small. Dad came in, still smiling. He looks like a movie star, everybody always says, and he's originally from Ireland, so he's got that whole accent thing going. Plus he's six foot three, with high cheekbones, dark brown wavy hair, and little lines coming off his eyes that make him look like he's hearing something funny. He sat beside me on the floor and said, "Gotta learn to take a joke, Maggie." He calls me Maggie. His voice is sort of hoarse, always, like he's been cheering too much.

"I can take a joke," I assured him.

He winked at me. "That's my girl." I used to love when he said that. He whispered, "We have enough sensitive types in this house, hey?" and raised his eyebrows toward the living room where Ned and Mom were still eating.

"Right," I whispered back.

"Well, then," he said, pointing at my feet. "Let's have a look."

I stood up to show him my turn-out. My feet just naturally face opposite walls.

"And that's good for ballet dancing, is it?"

I shrugged and made a face like, isn't that the funniest? But it is good for ballet, and all the other girls had gathered around me to look at my feet at the end of dance class that afternoon. I waited for his opinion on my blessed feet.

"Just looks like a duck to me," he said and smiled at me, though I saw a little questioning look in his eyes.

I forced my face into an imitation of a smile. "Quack," I said.

He swooped me up in his arms and said, "Come eat your supper, Duckie." I could tell he was proud I didn't have such easily bruised feelings as Mom. If he'd told her she looked like a duck, there'd be broken dishes and tears, for sure.

A few weeks before my eighth birthday, a tooth wiggled. I worked on it endlessly and showed Roxanne its progress every morning on our way to school. It hung by a thread for about a week. Roxanne offered to yank it out, but I felt a little queasy about that.

Ned and I were watching a video on my parents' bed one afternoon when they'd gone out to finish their fight. Mom was angry at Dad about something, he was being selfish again like always, she was being oversensitive, stuff was starting to be thrown, and they'd decided to take it outside.

Ned's eyes were narrow as they left, like they always got when Mom and Dad started fighting. He can't handle tension. I followed him into Mom and Dad's room where he turned on a movie with lots of punching.

I jumped on Ned to tackle him, get him to play with me, and my tooth fell out. We found it on his shirt.

He was in sixth grade and very cool at that point. I was jumping around like I'd just won a trip to Disney World. "Finally! My tooth! Yes!"

Without looking away from the guys beating each other up on the TV, Ned asked, "So what? You don't believe in the tooth fairy, do you?"

I stopped jumping and looked down at the tooth between my finger and thumb. I remember not wanting to answer. Even in second grade I had this idea I shouldn't make a fool of myself.

"The tooth fairy is just Mom and Dad, you know," he said.

"It is not."

"Trust me," he said and turned up the volume.

"Roxanne is friends with her."

"Roxanne is a liar," he said. "It's Mom."

That really bugged me. "It IS NOT! It's the tooth-freaking-fairy!" Ned and all his buddies used to put freaking in the middle of where it didn't belong all the time back then, and it sounded really tough and grown up to me.

I guess it didn't sound so tough to Ned, because he fell off the bed, laughing. "The tooth-freaking-fairy! I love it!"

"You shut up!" I yelled. I stood there stomping my feet, searching for any power to hold over him other than the obvious little-sister weapon. I had nothing, so out it came: "Shut up or I'm telling!"

"Tell," Ned answered.

"I will." I touched my tongue to the soft metallic-tasting space where the tooth used to be. Ned clicked off the TV. "Or don't tell. Don't tell them you lost your tooth at all. Just put it under your pillow and see if the tooth fairy really does show up."

"She will." I inspected the tooth. It looked weird and not very toothlike, with the roots showing there between my fingers. "Roxanne knows her."

"Right. Tell you what. If the tooth fairy does come," Ned said, "I'll match what she gives you."

"Fine," I said, close to tears, because the truth was, I had my doubts. Why would a fairy be willing to pay for such an ugly thing? And what was she planning to do with it, after? Roxanne had said something about jewelry, but it didn't make much sense. You could just use beads and not spend every night sneaking into kids' bedrooms.

"Let me see it," my brother asked. He held out his

hand. I placed the small, slightly bloody tooth softly inside.

"Psych!" he yelled and closed his fingers around the tooth. He lifted his fist above his head. I jumped, but Ned was already close to six feet. He ran around to the other side of my parents' bed.

I chased him, screaming, "Give it back! It's mine!"

"Not anymore!"

He ran out of their room. I followed him. He ran through the kitchen to the basement door, which he slammed shut behind him. I grabbed a metal spatula off the counter, flung the door open, and screamed, "Get up here!"

I was afraid of the basement, and my brother knew it. There was no light switch at the top of the stairs. You had to go down into the darkness and hold your arm up, wandering around without seeing, hoping the string hanging somewhere in the middle would brush your hand. My parents were always saying they should get a switch put in, but they never did.

No answer from Ned.

"Get up here!" I screeched. "Now!" I stomped as hard as I could on the top step, but the only effect was pain wavering up through my leg. I was holding the spatula up in the air like a weapon, although I had no idea if he could see me. I felt fierce; I wanted to kill him. It was *my* tooth, my first shot at getting something under my pillow from the tooth fairy. He was stealing from me. "Now!" I repeated with as much authority as I could muster.

When there was no response, I flung the spatula down into the darkness and slammed the door shut.

I heard a whimper, or thought I did, but I was scared he was just teasing me. I touched the doorknob, trying to decide what to do, whether or not to open it. I let go, then grabbed it again, and felt it turn in my palm.

The door opened. When I saw my brother, I fell back into the stove. There was blood pouring down into his eyes and he was crying, my big, tough hulk of a brother. I could see his forehead pulling apart from itself and shut my eyes tight against seeing his brains.

"Call 911!" he screamed, wiping blood out of his eyes.

Instead I opened the back door and ran away.

I was too scared to run far, so I just ran to my cherry tree and sat on the far side of it. My father found me out there later while Ned and Mom were at the hospital getting Ned's head sewn up.

"I thought you ran away," Dad said, his back against the bark, like mine.

"I did," I told him.

"Oh, Maggie," he said, laughing.

"What?"

"You're just like your old man, you know that?" He took me inside and gave me ice cream.

After everyone was asleep that night, I went down to the basement in my nightgown. I took about an hour getting down the dark steps, gripping the banister tight, telling myself if there are no fairies, then certainly there are no monsters, nothing to be scared of in the dark. *No such thing*, I said to myself before each step. *No such thing.* When there were no more stairs, I felt relieved, until I realized there was also no more banister to hold. I was adrift in the middle of the darkness, and in my imagination there were now pools of my brother's blood on the floor waiting to drown me in revenge for what I'd done. Only the fact that I wanted that first lost tooth so bad kept me going, hand raised, feet shuffling. I gasped when the string tickled my palm.

I closed my eyes and pulled the string, then got down on my knees on the cold concrete floor to search for my tooth. I found it pretty quickly and ran up the stairs. I was wasting a lot of money, leaving the light on, but at that point I was like, too bad; no way was I making the trip up in the dark. I ran to my room, placed the tooth under my pillow, and lay there in the bed with a pounding heart waiting for the tooth fairy. When I woke up, of course, the tooth was still there under my pillow. I hadn't really believed in her so much anyway.

Only babies believe in magic and fairies and stuff, I told myself, and put my tooth into a little white box because nobody would want it. Even my own body had no use for it anymore. When Mom noticed it was missing a few days later, she asked, "Why didn't you put it under your pillow, Morgan? For the tooth fairy!"

"Come on, Mom," I said, shaking my head. "I'm too old for stuff like that."

"You're seven."

I shrugged. "I don't even know what I did with it."

She looked really disappointed, walking away from me with slumped shoulders into the kitchen.

The next weekend, when Dad's friends came over to watch soccer on TV, he'd told them all how I'd split my brother's head open and run away. "Way to handle pressure, Maggie!" he said. "Yeah, when the going gets tough, run away and hide—that's my girl!"

My mother frowned and said, "Eddie."

"Don't be such a party pooper," he told her. Then he scooped me up into his lap to watch the game with him and his buddies.

five

I put the tooth in my Sack to show that part of me, the part that knows there's no such thing as magic. I was born a realist, not all sentimental like CJ, with her pink room and a flowered scrunchie on her bun. It's amazing she and I stayed friends as long as we did, come to think of it. We're so different.

She knows about what I did to Ned, though, so if I get up there and pull out this spatula, I know she'll cover her mouth and open her eyes wide like she did when I told her about it. She wanted to hear every detail, even the blood part. It made me feel tough, telling her about it; not ashamed, like I was some violent jerk, but tough and strong, the way Roxanne had seemed to me. When CJ and I played together, I got to make up the rules.

Well, that's over with, I guess, and who cares, because it's not like we play anymore. We're a little beyond that, or at least I am. If I get called and take out this spatula, she might think I'm gross. She might have changed her mind about me. I could say I'm into cooking or something, I guess.

CJ hasn't budged. It's beyond me how somebody can sit that straight and that still. Doesn't her behind start to itch, so bony on the hard chair?

Mrs. Shepard makes a clicking noise with her tongue, or maybe it's the pointy toe of her shoe tapping on the cold tile floor. I don't know. I don't want to look at her and give her an idea to call on me. I need time to come up with a bunch of lies about what my things symbolize.

"Louis Hochstetter," Mrs. Shepard calls.

Thank you. The boy can talk, which gives me a few seconds to think. Lou stands up abruptly behind me, jolting his chair into Zoe Grandon's desk. I would normally turn around and smile at Zoe about Lou's clumsiness, but not today. Zoe is my enemy, now.

Instead I take the opportunity to jiggle stuff around in my bag. The spatula CJ would recognize, and the ballet slipper, oh, dread, I can't let her see that. This can't be happening. The branch she might get or not, I don't know. I can't make a fool of myself in front of her and everybody; what am I going to say? I should've walked out with Roxanne. Oh, please, somebody help me.

My hand touches the cold, smooth medal. She won't recognize this. I never told her about this; she doesn't even know it exists. I clasp it in my hand, under my desk, as Lou Hochstetter scuffs by. *Saint Christopher, protect us.*

six

The day my father announced he was leaving was the Saturday after Fourth of July, three-and-a-little years ago. It had been sort of a rough year because Ned was being totally impossible, fighting at school and getting suspended, cursing at my mother, and threatening everybody who looked at him funny. Mom dragged him from one psychiatrist to another and read a hundred books on how to cope with him. She tried everything from putting us all on a macrobiotic diet to praising Ned every time he took a breath: *I appreciate that you didn't use very many curses in that sentence, Ned!*

Dad and I played catch in the backyard a lot that year. We didn't like to be in the middle of all that tension. He also started being a daily communicant, going to Mass every morning at seven. I heard Mom proudly telling a friend of hers on the phone that my father was able to handle things so well, able to turn to God and be a calming presence for the family.

I turned to God, too, wanting to be holy like my father. He wouldn't let me go to Mass with him every day, but on Sundays I would pray to Saint Christopher with all my might. *Saint Christopher, protect us*, I would say, my hands gripping each other tight as I knelt beside my father in the pew. *Saint Christopher, protect us*, because I had read that on my father's medal, the one he put on every morning as soon as he came out of the shower. I'd sneak in while he was showering to touch it. Down on my knees, I'd run my fingers over the raised saint's face on the front like getting my morning blessing: *Saint Christopher, protect us*. Then I'd quickly run back to my room so nobody would catch me being so corny.

That Fourth of July had been pretty disastrous, I guess, though at the time it had felt just sort of normal for us. We'd all gone to the fireworks at the high school, and Ned wanted to spread the blanket on the parking lot side because it would be louder there, and Mom was like, *No, let's go on the grass where it's more comfortable and not as loud*. Well, it turned into this huge thing, the two of them pulling the blanket like tug-of-war, when Dad yelled, "Who cares? Why do you two have to fight about everything?" Everybody turned around and looked at us. I was standing behind Dad's leg. He stands with his legs spread far apart and his feet turned out.

"Eddie," Mom stage-whispered.

"Oh, please," he said and walked away from them, mumbling, "I'm so sick of being the bad guy."

I ran after him. He stopped and knelt down to look me in the face. "Go back to Mom," he said.

"I want to go with you."

He smiled his winningest smile at me, I remember it. "I'll kiss you when you're sleeping. Go back to Mom now." He turned me and gave me a little shove on my back. A firework exploded over my head, startling me. I ran back to where Mom and Ned had been. They weren't there. I wandered around all through the show until I found them during the grand finale on the blanket in the parking lot.

The next Saturday, Mom stood alone in the kitchen while Dad had a talk with me and Ned. He told us this whole story of how the past few weeks he'd been driving around from construction-site inspection to construction-site inspection, as he'd always done, but realizing he didn't know who he was. "I can't recognize myself," were his words. "I don't know who I am."

"You're just Dad," I reminded him. "You're Eddie Miller."

I thought maybe he was losing his memory or his mind. I hoped Mom was in the kitchen calling a doctor. Ned sat beside me on the couch with his arms crossed and no expression on his broad, stony face.

"No, Maggie," Dad said. "I mean, I'm having some problems, inside myself. I'm having a problem with God. It's hard to explain, or understand. But what I think I have to do is get away for a while."

I shook my head. "Where?"

"What I've always dreamed of being is a movie actor."

"Really?" I asked.

"When I was a kid, my father lost his job and next thing, he's dragging the lot of us across the world— I'd never been outside County Cork before. Right? I was just a kid, sixteen years old, when I got here, knowing nothing and nobody. Your mother taught me to play cards and chew gum and next thing I knew I was a father myself, with a wife and a couple of kids and my summer construction job is suddenly my career, and it just feels, I'm choking. I honestly feel like I'm suffocating. So I have to go. I have to, Maggie, before I just, until I, well, I have to go find myself.

I can't be a very good father, can I be, if I don't know who I am?"

"What a ludicrous excuse," Mom said, poking her head out from the kitchen. "For their sake, I'm trying to keep my thoughts to myself, but come on, Eddie. Movie actor? You never acted in a single . . . you wouldn't come see me in the high school play! You said it was for zips, acting!"

Dad sighed. "Jo? You don't have an ambition, you don't have a gift—so you don't have any access to what I'm going through. Right?"

Mom stormed back into the kitchen. We heard cabinet doors slamming.

I tried desperately to think of something to say to ease Dad's pain. "Maybe we should talk to Father Connolly," I suggested. It honestly never occurred to me that this was anything more or less than my father having a mental meltdown.

Dad reached over and touched my cheek lightly. "I need to go," he said in his gravelly voice. He licked his lower lip.

"When?" asked Ned.

"I'll get my things together tonight, leave for Los Angeles first thing tomorrow morning."

Ned shrugged. "Go."

I don't remember the rest of that night so clearly, except I know I made a royal pain of myself, crying, begging, yelling at Mom not to let him go, hanging on his legs, screaming at Ned that it was his fault Daddy was leaving. I was pretty awful. Ned locked himself in his room, so I locked myself in mine but sat against the door listening to Mom and Dad. I fell asleep sitting there and woke up with a jolt at four the next morning. I raced to the living room—Dad was snoring on the couch, his feet hanging off the armrest. His two suitcases were by the front door.

I tiptoed over to my father and watched his beautiful, stubbly face as he slept. I resisted the temptation to snuggle under the blanket with him. His Saint Christopher medal lay inside the circle of his watch, its chain gathered in loops beneath it. I picked it up, knelt beside the coffee table, and began praying: *Saint Christopher, protect us. Don't let my daddy fall apart and have to go find himself in California. I love him so much. Give him the strength to stay with us, or give me the power to make him stay.*

And then Saint Christopher answered, "You have the power."

"What?" I whispered. I opened my eyes like, no way. I didn't really believe in stuff like that. I checked around to see if it was Ned, messing with me, but his door was still closed, so I looked down at the medal in my palm. It was warm, suddenly—not hot like I'd burn myself but warm like my father's hand.

OK, I thought, feeling excited but foolish. Dad never leaves the house without this thing. I closed my hands around the medal. *Thank you, Saint Christopher,* I whispered, getting up off my knees and tiptoeing back to my room. *Good, Morgan,* I whispered to myself on the way. *Talking to a necklace. You're losing it just like your father.*

I first put my father's necklace under my pillow, but then realized, no, he could find it there too easily, so I took my pillow out of the case and unzipped it. Inside were down feathers. I shoved my hand in with the Saint Christopher medal gripped tight and let go. I zipped the pillow back up and wiggled it back into my Minnie Mouse pillowcase. I fell asleep so soundly I didn't hear the commotion when my father woke up and searched.

From what Ned told me after, Dad tore the house apart looking for it, even accused Ned of stealing it, which led to a fight between Mom and Dad and then Mom and Ned, during which Dad took off. Mom says my father kissed me good-bye while I was sleeping; Ned says he didn't. Not that I care.

The Saint Christopher medal was cold when I dug it out of my pillow this weekend to put in my Bring Yourself in a Sack.

seven

Lou Hochstetter is explaining the differences between two miniature World War II guns. At least my stuff isn't as boring as his.

I let go of the Saint Christopher medal, let it drop into the bottom of my bag. It clanks into the envelope with the broken thermometer inside. I feel the thermometer, quick, to make sure it's OK, and then I look around to see if anybody is watching me hunt around inside my Sack. No. Everybody actually seems pretty wrapped up in Lou's speech about World War II artillery. I guess I'm just shallow.

eight

I went over to CJ's house for the first time in the fall of fourth grade. She seemed a little creepy, hardly ever talking, and so skinny her joints stuck out, but she invited me for a sleepover and since things were pretty grim at my house around then, I was happy to be anywhere else.

We played a few board games in the basement, and I showed her a card trick Ned had taught me.

"How did you do that?" she asked when her card appeared time after time.

"Magic," I said. That's what Ned told me a magician always says: Magic. You never give away the trick or you ruin it for the audience and it's not magic anymore.

CJ's green eyes opened wide. "Wow," she whispered.

I only knew the one trick so after a few times, when it was getting a little boring, I tried to teach CJ to play gin rummy. She couldn't hold ten cards in her tiny hands, though, and although we were only in fourth grade I had already outgrown seven-card gin. Anyway, I don't think CJ was too into cards. We put them away in their cardboard box on her playroom shelf and went out into her garden where her father was planting tulips. We stood at the edge of the flower bed for a few minutes, watching him press the dirt gently around the tulip bulbs. He looked up after a few, smiled at us, and asked if we wanted to help. CJ shrugged and looked at me. I wanted to. "I don't care," I said. "I guess."

Mr. Hurley let us each choose a bulb. I chose red, CJ chose yellow, though that was just predictions, on their boxes, of what color they'd turn out; right then they just looked like knobby onions. I held mine in my cupped palm, trying to imitate the way CJ was cradling hers, and forced myself not to brush the dirt off.

We placed them gently in holes next to each other, and Mr. Hurley checked to make sure enough soil was packed around each. We'd done a great job, he said, and told me I should remember where I planted mine so in the spring when I came back I could check on it. He said it could be mine. I shrugged, OK, like it was no big deal having my own red tulip in somebody else's garden. It was the third one in, second row.

I sort of wanted to keep pressing dirt around my tulip's roots, but Mr. Hurley said he'd give us a ride around the yard in the wheelbarrow, and CJ jumped up, clapping. "Don't tell Mommy," Mr. Hurley whispered to CJ. "She'd kill me." We climbed in quietly and carefully, but when Mr. Hurley lifted the handle, CJ and I tumbled onto our backs. He ran around the yard making quick turns, toppling us over until we were covered with dirt and scrambled up in each other's arms and legs, which made me laugh but also almost cry at the same time.

Her dad is sort of scrawny and has a thick mustache, the kind of man my own father would call a zip—as in "zero." Mr. Hurley made screeching noises while he charged around the yard with us screaming in the wheelbarrow, and also he did this thing with CJ where he'd grab her head in the crook of his elbow and look away from her at the same time, then when she was snuggled in against him, his arm encircling her head, he'd kiss her on the hair. He did it twice in that one afternoon, once in the flower bed and once after. Mrs. Hurley yelled out the window for us to get out of the wheelbarrow, we could get hurt.

I kept thinking maybe he would do it to me, too, but he didn't, even though I was standing right next to CJ when he did it the second time, and he easily could've grabbed me up, too. It would've felt weird anyway, probably, so it's good he didn't. I'm not the cuddly type. Even when I was a baby, I couldn't stand to be cuddled, my mother says; when my brother was a baby she never put him down, but I would scream whenever she held me until she left me alone with a toy in my bouncy seat. That's what she says, anyway. I don't remember that. I guess Mr. Hurley could tell I'm not the cuddly type. That's why he didn't cuddle me when he could've. Also it's not like we really knew each other well or anything.

After that, while Mr. Hurley, breathing heavy and sweating, set up the sprinklers, CJ and I went in her house to wash up. Mrs. Hurley was in the living room with CJ's little brother, Paul, who had a virus. She was spooning soup out of a bowl into his mouth. She suggested, after she made sure we hadn't gotten hurt with all that wildness outside, that we should play upstairs or in the basement again so we wouldn't bother Paul. His cheeks were rosy like they'd been slapped; he looked healthier than anybody else in the family, but I wasn't saying anything. It's not like I was part of their family. I followed CJ upstairs.

We washed our hands, then CJ showed me around. Her parents' room was peach-colored: peach wallpaper, peach wall-to-wall carpet, peach bedspread on a bed as big as my whole room. Below the window was a peach couch.

"A couch in the bedroom?" I asked CJ.

"It's a love seat," she said.

I shrugged like yeah, so what, I know that.

I'd never heard of a love seat before. It sounded like something private between a husband and wife, something maybe everybody knew about except stupid me. A love seat—the more I tried the words out in my head, love seat, love seat, the more it sounded like something kids shouldn't be allowed to see. My parents were separated but even before, they didn't have a love seat, or at least they didn't ever let me see their love seat.

"Let's go," I said, desperate to get away from staring at it.

CJ showed me her brother's room next. It was blue and white with a sports theme—the wallpaper border around the top had pictures of balls from every different sport. His comforter matched. In a big see-through hamper were real balls to match the pictures.

"Your brother must really like sports," I said.

"No," she answered. "He likes computers."

I took a Nerf football out of his hamper and followed CJ to the bathroom.

"This is the bathroom," she said.

"No kidding," I said.

She blushed, which made me feel guilty. In the car on the way to CJ's that morning, my mother had said, *Try to behave yourself, Morgan, and don't be too obnoxious.*

"Sorry" I told CJ. "Just kidding."

She smiled without showing her teeth and took me to her room. It was pink with a canopy bed and built-in shelves and a dressing table in the corner— the kind that has a long white skirt down to the floor, and you can sit on the thickly padded stool staring at your face in the heart-shaped mirror and swing the arms open so the see-through fabric brushes over your legs, and you can easily imagine you're somebody. I closed my eyes.

"Let's go back in your parents' room," I said.

"Why?"

"Have a catch." I held up her brother's football.

"We can't, inside," she said. "You want to go outside?"

I opened my eyes and saw her nervous face as pale as it could possibly ever get. *You spoiled brat*, I thought, hating her, wanting to punish her for showing off all her stuff like she thought she was so great just because she has a pink room with pink shelves holding more ceramic horses and Barbies on stands than any one girl could possibly need and a dressing table you could sit down at and be pretty.

"You scared?" I asked her, digging my fists into my hips.

She shook her head slightly. "No."

I turned and stalked into her parents' room and while I waited for her to follow me, I let myself check out the love seat again. It just looked like a small couch, no matter how I tried to squint and imagine.

When I felt CJ behind me, I turned, backed up, and tossed her the Nerf football. She lunged for it. In ballet class, I always felt jerky and abrupt beside her, because she moved so smoothly. Going for the ball, though, her body didn't seem to know what it was doing. She bent her knees in a deep *plié* to catch it and pushed her chin way out front, I don't know why. It made me like her again, seeing her so awkward, and her little relieved smile when she opened her eyes and discovered the football in her arms made me want to be gentle to her.

"Good catch," I said.

CJ lifted her spindly arm high above her head to

toss the ball back to me. She squeezed her eyes shut before flinging the ball. It wobbled sideways off her fingers. I rushed toward it, but before I could make a grab, the ball had smashed into the stuff on top of her parents' dresser.

CJ gasped when she opened her eyes after the crashing sound. I was already in front of the dresser lifting the Nerf ball off the clutter of perfume bottles and cuff links.

"It's OK," I told her.

She stood behind me, panting, her long, skinny fingers pulling at her lips. "What's that?" she whispered.

"Mercury," I said and picked up a broken piece of glass, which had been part of a thermometer. "A thermometer broke." When I turned to show it to her, I discovered I'd been wrong—she actually could get paler.

"My, my, brother's, temperature. My mother doesn't, trust, the el-el-electronic . . ."

"It's OK," I whispered again, worrying she might faint. "We'll clean it up. They'll never know."

"I'm n-n-n-not, not, not . . ." She backed away from me until she bumped into the love seat and sat down on the edge of it, her posture erect except for her dropped head, which was clutched between her hands. I liked her for that, how guilty she felt even if I also thought she was being a little babyish. It just seemed to me like somebody who would feel all guilty and bad about herself for breaking a thermometer is someone you could trust not to be selfish. Selfish was a big word in my house that year.

I pulled a tissue out of the peach-colored ceramic tissue box holder. "I'll just clean it," I assured her. "See?"

She peeked up over her hands. I grabbed a big wad of mercury with the tissue and tried to hold it up to show her.

"See? I asked again, but as I asked, the mercury broke into two balls and escaped, jumping back down to the dresser. "Hey!" I said to it and heard CJ sort of giggle. It was more like a huff of air, actually, but I could tell it was the Cornelia-Jane-Hurley version of a giggle. "Get over here!" I whispered, grabbing again at the escaping blob. "Get! You! Get over here!"

She still had her fingers over her mouth, but she was definitely laughing, and I remember deciding right at that second that I wanted to be best friends with her. She has the quietest little squeak of a laugh. I remember how surprised I was to hear it, because she didn't laugh much, not in school, definitely never in ballet class. She almost never talked, even—just stared with those deep-set green eyes in her pale, hollowed-out face. But when she giggled, hiding her mouth and perching on the edge of the love seat in her perfect, huge house, well, she made me want to protect her and hear another tiny little private squeaking giggle. So I chased around the balls of mercury on her parents' dresser more than I really needed to. I could've caught them, but I kept letting them escape, to prolong her laughter.

She took a deep breath and dropped her head back into her hands. "I'm in such big trouble," she whispered. "When my mom finds out . . ."

"She won't," I told her.

CJ looked up at me again.

"I'll clean the whole thing up and bring the pieces home with me," I said. "Your mom will think she just lost it. She never has to know."

We stared at each other for a few seconds. Finally CJ whispered, "Really?"

I shrugged like, no big deal, and then out of my mouth popped, "You're my best friend."

I hadn't meant to say it like that. It was our first sleepover, and I had no way of knowing if she even liked me at all, and there I was blurting that she's my best friend. I couldn't think of what to do, so I grabbed for another ball of mercury and said, *Get!* But it wasn't that funny anymore.

"You're my best friend, too," CJ whispered.

We smiled at each other. What a relief. "I'll never tell anybody about the broken thermometer," I promised her, quickly gathering up the pieces in tissues. "Don't worry. You won't get in trouble. I'll bring the pieces home with me, and no one will ever know. Even on my deathbed, I'll never tell."

"Thank you," she whispered back.

After I got up all the little shards of glass and wrapped them in layers of tissues, we tiptoed down to the kitchen to tape it into a tight tissue ball and hide it in my suitcase. Mrs. Hurley was reading to Paul. She called to us and asked if we needed anything. CJ held on to my sleeve and said, "No!" We waited a few seconds, then smiled slowly at each other.

We brought my suitcase, with its secret inside, up to CJ's pink room, where we played Barbies for a few hours. I didn't have any Barbies at my house, because my mother thinks they're sexist and perpetuate bad stereotypes and unrealistic body images that are damaging to young girls. CJ's mother I guess thought they were OK. I sat cross-legged in the middle of CJ's floor and wiggled my fingers deep into her pale pink carpet.

CJ took down all the Barbies from her shelf and let me choose whichever I wanted, even her newest one. I would probably have said, *You can choose any except this one, because I just got her.* But not CJ. She even let me dress the new Barbie in the bridal gown. The Barbie CJ chose had to be the groom, because CJ had no Kens. She shrugged and said, "That's OK," and I knew then that I had made a really good choice. I was only nine, but I knew already that most people aren't about to let you be the bride.

nine

I look at the sealed white envelope in my brown bag while Lou Hochstetter finishes his presentation. I touch the envelope with my fingers, feeling the piece of thermometer inside.

I've kept the wadded-up pieces in my top desk drawer since I got home from CJ's the next day and never told a single person, not ever. The first time I even took it out of the drawer was when I got that phone message from CJ, Friday afternoon. I cut the Scotch tape and spread the tissues out on my desk. I chose the biggest piece of thermometer off the tissues and slipped it into an envelope and put the envelope into the brown paper bag that had been standing open and empty on top of my desk blotter. I wondered for a second, *What will Mrs. Shepard think, a broken thermometer?* But she never said anything about you have to choose things that are obvious why you chose them; the assignment was: Choose ten things that represent who you are in all your many facets. So I thought, *Too bad if she doesn't know the meaning. This is who I am.* And not even just, *I'm best friends with CJ Hurley,* but also, *I can keep a secret and never tell.*

I slip the envelope with the thermometer inside it into my desk, now.

No way can I get up in front of everybody and say, *This broken thermometer is a symbol that I'm best friends with CJ,* because now I'm not. She doesn't want me anymore. Not that I care. It's just, now I have only nine things left in my bag and what if Mrs. Shepard calls me?

I could say, *And my tenth thing is nothing, which symbolizes the friendship ring I don't have.* Sure. Like I would ever say anything so embarrassing.

Lou's guns and tanks from World War II are spread across Mrs. Shepard's desk. He's been smiling at Mrs. Shepard, but she hasn't said Fine. She's pointing her tongue at her upper lip, all four and a half solid feet of her waiting for something. Poor goofy Lou is starting to sweat. I think she hates him. "And?" she finally asks.

"And?" he asks back.

"And what does this panoply of World War II armaments reveal about Louis Hochstetter?"

Lou rubs his pants leg with the work boot on his other foot. "What do you mean?" Most social studies teachers go crazy for Lou and his expertise. We've been hearing variations of his World War II lectures for the past four years.

Mrs. Shepard narrows her eyes slightly. "The assignment, Mr. Hochstetter."

We all wait. My hand is inside my brown paper bag, but I'm too terrified to move it, even to pull it out. Nobody moves, except our eyes—from her to Lou, who is resting his weight on his palm, beside his carefully arranged but suddenly ridiculous-looking World War II toys.

"The purpose of this assignment," Mrs. Shepard states quietly, "was to reveal yourself in all your various aspects. Have you done that, Mr. Hochstetter?"

"I, sort of," Lou managed. His face is turning purple.

"Oh?" Mrs. Shepard raises her eyebrows and I realize my mouth is hanging open.

Lou takes a big breath and bravely stutters, "I'm interested in, in World War II. Armaments."

"Is that interest all there is to Louis Hochstetter?"

Lou's eyes look misty. "Pretty much," he answers.

What if she calls me next? No way am I standing there like poor Lou, ready to blubber. I have to think of something to split in half, fast.

Mrs. Shepard waits what feels like forever before she says, "Hmm."

Lou places his guns and tanks gently back into his brown bag. I can't watch. I turn my head, and who's looking at me? CJ. She sits right next to me. We shake our heads at each other and make sad faces. Pour Lou. He's a total zip but still. CJ closes her eyes, opens them slowly, and smiles slightly at me.

Maybe I've misunderstood.

My fingers are freezing cold. *OK, OK. Concentrate because I could be called next.* The cards, I could split them up. My mother's gray, worn deck of cards that I'm never supposed to take out of the leather case in her night table drawer. I could pull two cards and leave the rest, bound by the rubber band, in my desk. Which two? A queen of diamonds because I love jewelry (too bad if I don't) and a joker because I'm so funny? Right. Oh, God, I'm in big trouble.

I could put in the black scrunchie I have around my wrist. Oh, that's meaningful. "To symbolize my hair." No. I push the spatula aside and the branch. What's in this box? I open it stealthily, under my desk, inside the bag. Oh, yeah. My baby tooth. Maybe I could say the box means something? What? A little white box. Because I'm interested in little white boxes. Sure.

I turn again to my left. CJ is still looking at me, making that sad face as Lou crosses in between us, shuffling back to his seat. She raises her hand to her neck, her sign for being scared or sympathetic. I do the same thing. She smiles.

I definitely must've misunderstood what happened this morning. She still wants to be best friends. Of course she does.

"Gabriela Shaw," says Mrs. Shepard. CJ and I both breathe a sigh of relief. I almost touch my nose with crossed fingers, our symbol for being best friends, but at the last second I stop myself. My fingers lie crossed on top of the brown bag as I try to decide what's really going on.

CJ said, right before lunch, that it wasn't what I thought. I just didn't let her explain what happened this morning with her and Zoe Grandon. It must all be a misunderstanding. I'm just stupid. Hallelujah.

I don't even care what Gabriela has to say. I roll my eyes at CJ, like, *I am such a jerk, I'm sorry*. I make a show of looking into my bag, then flaring my nostrils like the stuff inside stinks. CJ hunches her shoulders and smiles.

ten

After our first sleepover, CJ and I were practically inseparable. We ate lunch together, and whispered all day in school, and of course took ballet together. Me, CJ, and this girl Fiona were the best in the class; the other girls watched us three warm up in a tight threesome. But even Fiona knew CJ and I were best friends. Our two mothers car-pooled. After ballet we'd go back to one house or the other, depending on whose mother picked up, and spend all afternoon.

One afternoon we were at my house. When Mrs. Hurley came to pick up CJ, Mom was looking for an excuse to delay writing her college applications. "Let them finish playing," she said to Mrs. Hurley. "How about some coffee?"

Mrs. Hurley smiled and said, "Terrific." Mrs. Hurley looks like a model. Beautiful people, like my father, really intimidate Mom. She took out her best cups, the ones she inherited from her parents, the ones we never touch.

CJ and I were in the middle of appearing together on an imaginary talk show in my room. We were telling the audience of my stuffed animals how it felt to be the two prettiest and most accomplished prima ballerinas in the world, how there was never, no, we swear it, not a shred of jealousy between us, we just took turns dancing every lead. It wouldn't be any fun touring the world without each other, we insisted into the empty roll of toilet paper we were using as a microphone.

"Oh, yes, there are differences," I told the cardboard roll. "CJ has the longer neck."

CJ grabbed the mike and insisted that I had better turn-out, perfect.

I shrugged humbly and pointed my toes toward opposite sides of my room. The stuffed animals lined up on my bed clapped as we broke for a commercial. Since one of the three doors in my bedroom goes to the kitchen, CJ and I used the break from being interviewed to crouch behind it and eavesdrop on our mothers. I remember it so clearly, smiling at each other as we held in our giggles in anticipation of hearing some juicy grown-up gossip.

My mother was whispering about what an immature jerk my father was—her favorite subject those days (these, too). "So he felt that he didn't know who he was. I told him, You are the father of two children, that's who you are."

CJ's mom whispered back, "That's right."

"But he left." My mother's voice cracked like she might cry. "The next morning, he packed the car and left."

I heard Mrs. Hurley gasp sympathetically, then the coffeepot clink against a cup. My eyes were closed, and I don't know about CJ, but giggles were no longer a problem for me.

"Now he's in L.A. bumming around, being a starving actor," I heard my mother continue.

"Really?" asked Mrs. Hurley.

"Don't even get me started," Mom replied. I prayed to Saint Christopher with clenched fists and eyes that Mrs. Hurley wouldn't get her started.

"Los Angeles?" Mrs. Hurley asked, like that was the unbelievable part. I peeked up at CJ. Her face was buried in her lap.

My mother laughed her cough of a laugh and said, "Los Angeles. And meanwhile I don't have enough money to buy tuna fish, never mind ballet lessons. They've sent me three notices, and I just got a message on the machine that they'll turn Morgan away from class this week if I don't bring the money, which I don't have."

"Oh, my gosh," Mrs. Hurley whispered. I remember her voice saying that, because I had never heard that expression before and thought it was a really bad curse, the way she whispered it: Oh, my gosh. My mother is so clueless to tell some lady she barely knew about her financial troubles. She sounded like such a kid. She sounded like she was in desperate need of a grown-up to take over. I was only nine, but who else was there?

I pushed open the door to the kitchen. Mrs. Hurley was so startled when the door slammed into the corner of the table, she splashed her coffee all over her white sweater. *Too bad*, I thought. She stood up. My mom stood up, too, and grabbed one paper towel, which wasn't nearly enough.

I turned to my mother and said, "I hate ballet."

"Morgan," she said to me, then smiled at Mrs. Hurley. "I have a Stain Stick that'll get that spot right off your sweater. I'm so sorry. Let me just . . ."

"Seriously!" I yelled, grabbing the dish towel that hung on the stove and shoving it toward Mrs. Hurley. "I hate it! It's stupid and boring. If I could quit I'd be the happiest person."

Tears were starting, so I had to turn away from the mothers. When I did, I was facing my room, where CJ was still sitting cross-legged, her face just slightly raised above her folded arms on top of her legs in their pale pink ballet tights.

"CJ wants to quit, too," I said. Her pointy face turned as green as her eyes. "She hates it as much as I do, don't you? CJ? She told me. She's just afraid to admit it!"

Mrs. Hurley dragged CJ out of our puny house as fast as she could. She didn't even finish dabbing at her sweater. Mom chased them down the driveway, offering Stain Stick.

I locked myself in the bathroom. My mother knocked on the bathroom door and said, "You sure have a gift for stopping conversation dead."

I wasn't in much of a joking mood. "At least I have a gift."

"Hey!" She opened the door and found me crouched on the floor. "You can shut your smart mouth, miss."

I hadn't meant to say it like that, like my father. I just meant, Leave me alone. So I explained, "Nothing personal."

"No?" She stood over me, with her fists on her hips, which made her look solid and fierce, although she's only five foot one, like I am now.

"Just," I said, "I'm happy you think I have a gift."

Mom sneered. "It wasn't meant as a compliment."

I said, "No kidding." We had a really charming relationship at that point. Not that it's about to win the congeniality prize now.

She whirled around, stomped out of the bathroom, through my room, and out of the living room, slamming doors behind her. I sat in there by myself for a while after that. I think I might even have taken a bath, but that might be my imagination. Anyway, the next thing I remember I was standing at her bedroom door, and it was late that night, and I was asking if she wanted to play gin.

She loved playing gin; I had fallen asleep so many nights listening to her and Dad flipping cards onto the table. They had fun when they did that, I think.

"I hate seven-card gin," Mom grumbled. Her TV was on, and her covers were pulled up around her. There was a container of yogurt on her bedside table with a spoon in it.

"I can hold ten cards now," I said, holding up my hands to show how much they'd grown. I remember thinking, *Anything just don't hate me.*

"OK," she said and reached over to her night table where the cards always stayed, in the tight brown leather container my father had bought for her for Valentine's Day when they were in Boggs High together and madly in love.

"You want to see a card trick?" I asked her, thinking a little magic might cheer her up.

"Can we just play gin?"

"Sure," I said. "It's a stupid trick anyway."

We played a few hands. I dropped all my cards once. She didn't yell at me, just scooped them all up and said she'd had nothing, anyway, I'd done her a favor.

"You're welcome," I said. "Did you and Dad have a love seat?"

"What?"

"Nothing," I said quickly, turning to watch a deodorant commercial on her TV.

"Morgan?" She shuffled, making a bridge out of the cards that fluttered flappingly into a neat stack.

"Nothing!" I looked at her with my most adamant face.

She started to deal the cards. "About ballet . . ."

"I really do hate it," I answered as fast as I could. "Isn't it my deal?"

She scooped up the cards and handed me the deck. "Thank you," she whispered.

That's when *Little House on the Prairie* came on. We both turned to the TV and watched the opening. I forced myself to go back to playing cards. She'd been playing solitaire a lot; I'd heard the cards slapping on one another.

"You want to take a break and watch this dumb show?" she asked.

I shrugged. "Not really."

"So do I," she said.

She took the cards and slipped them back inside their leather case. I snuggled under the covers with her and we watched. We both agreed Michael Landon was so cute, his name should be Cutie. Toward the end of the show, he pulled up his horse-drawn buggy beside his daughter, Laura, and said he'd be done working soon and did she want to go fishin'?

Mom and I sunk down on her pillows.

"Wouldn't that be nice?" Mom asked.

"I hate fish," I reminded her.

"Yeah," she said. "And can you imagine having to go to the well so often?"

"And wear a hat to bed?"

We agreed we were way better off than the Ingalls family. I fell asleep in her bed that night, and I never put my ballet slippers back on. It just would've hurt Mom.

eleven

CJ didn't quit with me, obviously. This summer she made it up to performance level, which means she'll be taking five classes a week this year. She was so proud, I had to be happy for her, even if I couldn't help pointing out that she wouldn't be able to play soccer like all the normal people. I wonder if that annoyed her. But she knows I only mean it's fun to be inseparable, like we used to be. I thought she knew that.

She never told anybody the real reason I quit. She told Fiona I got bored of it, and Fiona can think whatever she wants, CJ stood by me. Fiona is such a boring bun-head, CJ and I always say. I had better turn-out than she did. She was jealous of that, and of my friendship with CJ. I could be on my way to prima ballerina, too.

Gabriela is showing her key chain and explaining how she has two homes, her mother's and her father's, and that it's hard for her—she has trouble keeping track of where her shoes are and knowing who to ask to sign her permission slip, but at least she gets to bring her cat back and forth with her. Everybody squirms, listening to this. It's too personal. Gabriela is really nice but so clueless.

twelve

Fifth grade, when I was turning eleven, was the first time Mom took the camera out and dragged me in front of my cherry tree to pose. I didn't want to; without Dad there it was just depressing. While she was positioning me, Ned muttered something about no cherries ever growing on my cherry tree and how my father had probably just bought the wrong kind.

Mom agreed. She said something like "defective" as she was trying to figure out the focus.

I yelled, "It is not defective!"

"Right," Ned said.

"It'll have cherries by next year on my birthday," I insisted, and Mom snapped the picture. I look angry in it.

"Don't get all worked up about it," Mom said. "Can we please? I have to set up for your party."

"It will," I said. "You'll see."

"Fifteen screeching kids on their way," Mom complained. "I can't deal with this today." She hurried inside to hang streamers.

"It will," I whispered again. Nobody was listening to me, so I got on my bike and rode for a while.

When I got back, my guests had already arrived and Mom was furious at me for running away. "Just like your father," she whispered. She gave me the Silent Treatment, all through my party.

The next weekend, I stole a bottle of vitamin-rich plant food out of Mr. Hurley's shed. Every Saturday morning before Ned and Mom woke up, I poured little capfuls around the tree's roots. I kept the bottle hidden under my bed, because I didn't want to explain. Mr. Hurley would never notice; he had three bottles of it all lined up in his gardening shed. Whenever I went over to CJ's, I watched him, how he watered and worried over his plants. I watered my cherry tree and walked around it, all that summer and fall. I even stopped checking my red tulip at the Hurleys, out of loyalty to my tree.

In the winter, last year, I did nothing, because Mr. Hurley did nothing. *Let it lie fallow*, he said, when I casually asked how do you help the garden in the winter. *Let it lie fallow,* he said, *let it rest so it can save its energy for the spring.* He asked if I was getting interested in gardening. I just shrugged and said not really.

When the snow melted, he went back to feeding his garden and worrying over it, so I started with the little capful and the watering again, too.

"Pacing around it isn't gonna make it grow cherries, you know," Ned unhelpfully told me.

"No kidding," I said, rolling my eyes. He thinks he's so brilliant.

By the end of March, there were blossoms all over the branches. Almost every morning before school, I woke up early, made myself some tea, forced myself to sit at the table and drink it, and then went out back before Mom and Ned stopped snoring. I climbed up my tree and checked for cherries.

Nothing.

At night I prayed. *Come on, Saint Chris,* I said, hoping friendliness might influence him. *One cherry. How hard can one little cherry be for a saint? I'm not asking for world peace here. A measly cherry, on a cherry tree. It's not for myself, Chris—it's for my mother, so she'll know my father didn't plant her a defective tree when I was born. She'd be so happy.*

Nothing.

Mom drank her coffee each morning standing in the kitchen, looking out the window at the tree, and I knew she was thinking, what a stupid defective tree. I watched her.

A month before my birthday, I told her one morning, "I think this might be the year we get cherries."

She shrugged. "I don't even like cherries that much anyway," she said.

"Yes, you do." I hiked myself up to sit on the counter. "You love cherries."

"Morgan, don't agitate me today, OK?" She spilled out the rest of her coffee. "Get off the counter. I have an exam tonight, and my boss is on my case, and I'm just way too stressed to be patient with your fantasies. OK? Like it or not, you play the hand you're dealt. This is our life, so we have to get used to it."

"I am used to it," I told her, still up on the counter.

"Good." She shoved her feet into her shoes and grabbed her keys off the hook. "So can we stop with wishing for cherries to magically appear?"

I quit praying for magic and came up with a plan.

I hoarded my allowance. We won a softball game that week, but I made up an excuse that I couldn't go to the pizza place after, had to ride right home, because I was grounded for cursing at my mother. A total lie—I just didn't want to waste the money on a slice of pizza. I needed it.

The day before my birthday, I limped around school saying I had hurt my ankle, so I'd get out of softball practice. I hobbled away from the gym, then jumped on my bike and rode to the grocery store, all my money in the pocket of my khaki shorts.

That night, Mom took me and CJ and Ned out to Red Lobster and said we could choose anything we wanted off the menu, including for dessert. CJ said she just wanted the shrimp cocktail. I don't know if she was trying to save my mother some money or just watching her weight as always. I almost ordered the same, but my mother looked so disappointed I chose a lobster. It was delicious. I got a sundae for dessert, and CJ tasted it. She was practically falling asleep on the table, because she'd had ballet that afternoon.

After we dropped CJ off, I raced into the house to check the messages and e-mail. Nothing. "I'm sure he'll call tomorrow," Mom whispered, trying to hug me.

"Who?" I asked, pulling away.

"Why do you always pull away from me?"

"I'm tired." I sat on the windowsill in my room with my face pressed against the glass, straining to see my tree, for a little while, then set my alarm for four-thirty A.M., checked the bag under my bed, and got under my covers.

The next morning I woke up just before the alarm buzzed. I think it must've clicked, because my eyes popped open and I slammed down the snooze button just as the buzz was starting. I flipped the switch to off, got out of bed, and pulled up the covers in one motion, and took the grocery bag out from under. I tiptoed to the kitchen, filled the teakettle with water, and climbed onto the counter to get a tea bag out of the box I'd hidden there. When the steam came out of the kettle, I poured it over the bag in my mug and watched the water darken. I dragged the tea bag around inside the mug and hummed "Happy Birthday" to myself.

"Happy Birthday to Morgan," I whispered, pouring in the milk and watching the cloudiness curl into itself. Humming the rest, I went out to sit at the table and drink my tea. No presents on the table. Big surprise. Well, I got dinner. And I don't need anything, I reminded myself. I wear my sandals every day it's warm enough, and I take good care of my clothes, and it's not like I played with toys or anything anymore, and I've never been the jewelry type. I finished my tea as quickly as I could, threw on some sweats, grabbed the grocery bag, and quietly, silently, opened the back door to step out into the cool.

The grass was damp under my sandals. I crossed our little yard quickly and left my sandals at the base of the tree, beside the grocery bag. I climbed up into a crook of the trunk, the plastic bag of cherries in my teeth and the roll of Scotch tape in my waistband. I had bought as many cherries as I could afford, almost four and a half pounds, which is a lot when your fingers are cold and the branches are a little damp so you have to wrap Scotch tape around and around each stem.

When I finished, it was six-fifteen. I climbed down and stood back, in the cold grass, to see. The branches hung heavy with fruit. One of them really drooped, where I'd overcrowded. It was beautiful. There were maybe a hundred cherries taped up there, but it looked like a thousand to me, with the sun coming up brightening the sky behind the tree. They looked like jewels. I grabbed the bag and my sandals and raced back inside, thinking, *This will show her,* and also, *I hope she likes it. She deserves a nice thing, and she really does love cherries.*

It felt like forever, lying there in my bed with my nightgown back on, waiting for Mom to get up. She hit her snooze three times, until I was ready to go clonk her over the head with the clock. After her alarm rang the fourth time, she grumbled and went into the bathroom. I heard the toilet flush and then the water running in the sink. She must've brushed every single tooth four hundred times, it felt like. Finally, she padded to the kitchen. The coffee beans were ground up noisily and water poured into the coffee machine. I buried my head in my pillow to keep from shouting, *Look out the window!*

I listened past the percolating of the coffee machine for any sound. Nothing. What was she doing in there? The fridge opened and closed. Look out the window! And then I heard it. A gasp.

I couldn't stand it anymore. I jumped up and raced into the kitchen, trying my best to look sleepy. "What?"

Her face was puffy, there was some mascara smudged under her eyes, her thick stack of curly hair was leaning toward the window. She looked beautiful. Her mouth was open but almost smiling. She didn't move, just stood there pointing out the window. "The! The!" she said. She shook her head a little and breathed out hard through a spreading smile.

"What?" I looked out the window, squinted like I couldn't see all those fat red cherries decorating the branches.

"I don't believe it," she whispered. "Cherries!" She blinked a few times, then grabbed me by the nightgown and dragged me out into the backyard.

I flopped behind her, trying not to smile.

"How in the world?" she whispered breathlessly as she pulled me barefoot across the lawn. "I never thought . . . Look at them, there must be a thousand cherries, I just yesterday looked and . . ."

She reached up to touch a deep red cherry, and

pulled. It didn't come off, so she pulled some more. Pulled and pulled and pulled. "What the . . . ?"

She yanked so hard the branch arched down to her waist, and when the cherry finally came off in her hand, there were loops of tape around the stem. She brought it up close to her face, then slowly raised her eyes to look at me. "Morgan," she said.

I squinted at the cherry. "Hmm. That's weird," I said.

"You taped cherries to the tree?" she asked.

I looked at my toes in the grass. "It must be magic," I mumbled.

"There must be twenty dollars' worth of cherries taped to this tree."

I smiled to myself but didn't say anything. It was eighteen, really.

"Oh, Morgan," she said, sighing.

"Taste it," I suggested.

"How will we ever get all these cherries off?"

I shrugged. "I guess the tree isn't defective, huh? We should call Dad."

She threw the cherry onto the grass. "Would you stop it already? He is the one who left, and I am sticking it out here. OK? Will you for once stop apologizing for him?"

"I didn't . . ."

"I am not mad at you," she said angrily, clutching

my shoulders. "Do you understand? I just don't know why you would do such a stupid thing."

As I walked back inside, I heard her asking again, "How am I supposed to get all these cherries down? They're all going to rot."

thirteen

"Thomas Levit," Mrs. Shepard calls. I guess I spaced out on the rest of Gabriela Shaw's presentation, because she's already sitting down. Tommy's chair screeches as he pushes it back. CJ's new boyfriend. So cute, the jerk.

Oh, no. The red-hots. What am I going to say about them? Because Tommy and CJ both will definitely recognize this box of red-hots in my bag.

I roll my eyes at CJ, she rolls hers back, and I'm feeling OK for the first time all day. So what if Tommy is going out with CJ? That's OK, I decide generously. She's my best friend. So I'll go out with Jonas; Jonas is sweeter than Tommy, and cute, in his own way, definitely. Jonas has rosy cheeks and long eyelashes, although he has started walking like a chicken. But I could get past that, probably. His twin, Tommy, looks nothing like him. Tommy has dark, straight hair hanging into his dark eyes, and he does this thing with his chin—he sort of points with it at you when he's including you in a joke. He juts his chin out and looks at you out of the corner of his eyes, then looks away. I don't know why that made me so crazy last year, but it did, and I went out with him for two weeks until I dumped him for being too horny. Since then we've been a little weird around each other.

But I'll get Zoe Grandon to ask Jonas if he likes me. CJ and I and the Levits will be a foursome anyway, just switch guys; best friends do that. It's fun. Zoe is taller than Jonas and Tommy, and last week she said herself she doesn't like either of them like that, just as friends. Zoe is a very friendly person. I have nothing against her. She's been president of our grade since there've been grade-wide elections. I've always voted for her. She smiles easily and laughs at any joke or wisecrack you make, and she genuinely seems to like everybody, which is beyond me. Nobody annoys her. She has stringy blond hair and huge blue eyes that focus only on whoever is talking to her, like she's got nowhere else she'd rather be.

CJ would never choose Zoe as a best friend. I don't

know what I was thinking this morning. Zoe's too, I don't know, big. Too happy. Too popular. No depth. I can't believe I was stupid enough to think CJ would dump me for Zoe—Zoe, with her huge grin and stringy hair and no depth. *Zoe's bag is probably empty*, I tell myself, and almost laugh out loud, having cheered myself up so thoroughly.

Then I remember my red-hots dilemma, and that gets me serious again fast. *What am I going to say about these red-hots?*

fourteen

Zoe fixed me up with Tommy Levit last year, in sixth grade. Everybody watched him ask me out, up on the upper playground. When he wandered over before school that morning in the snow, all the sixth-grade girls made squeaky noises and pushed me toward him, because, of course, Zoe had told everybody she was fixing us up. I could feel them all watching us walk toward the chain-link fence, through the already crunched-up snow.

When we got to the fence, he mumbled, "Will you?"

"OK," I said. Then we ran back to our separate groups of friends.

We didn't talk to each other the rest of that week

or the next, but Valentine's Day was the following Saturday, and there was a party at Zoe Grandon's house, which is right behind the Levits'. Pretty much everybody in sixth grade went. We didn't talk to each other much there, either, but at ten-thirty when we were all shrugging our soggy jackets on in the dining room, getting ready to leave, Tommy shoved a box of red-hots from his jacket pocket into mine. Taped to it was a note that said, "Happy V-Day. Tommy."

CJ and I were having a sleepover that night, after the party. We stayed up all night reading and rereading the note. We planned what would happen if Jonas asked her out and the four of us were a foursome all through middle school and high school. We planned to go on the seventh-grade apple-picking trip as two couples, discussing if we should sit with them or with each other on the bus, and maybe kissing them, there. That cracked us up, talking about kissing. We kept falling back on her bed, pretending to faint. *Do you think you have to move your face around*, she asked, imitating how people do it in the movies. We made kissy noises and then pulled the necklines of our nightgowns up over our chins, embarrassed, and agreed we were too young to have to worry about it.

We got out construction paper and markers and wrote, *Morgan and Tommy, CJ and Jonas. Morgan Levit and CJ Levit.* We decorated the papers with hearts and some glitter. *If we marry them someday,* we whispered, *we'll finally be real sisters, or at least sisters-in-law.* We crossed our fingers and touched our noses as we watched the sun rise.

By breakfast, CJ and I were exhausted but still giddy. We tore our artwork into tiny bits, then dialed the Levits' number like twenty times before I finally got my courage together and asked to speak to Tommy. It was nine-thirty on a Sunday morning, and his father sounded pretty groggy.

Tommy picked up the phone and asked, "Hello?"

"Hi."

"Who's this?"

"Morgan. Miller. From school." I rolled my eyes at CJ, who was pretzeled up inside her legs on her bed.

"Hi," Tommy said.

"Hi."

"What do you want?"

"Um . . ." I couldn't remember. "I just, thanks for the red-hots. They're delicious." I hadn't opened them. I still haven't.

"Oh," he said. "No big deal."

"Right," I agreed. "I didn't say it was."

"We're gonna build a snow fort," he said. "Me and Jonas."

"Oh, OK," I said, shaking my head at CJ like, why did you talk me into this? "'Bye, then."

"No," he said quickly. I raised my eyebrows; CJ leaned forward. Tommy finished, "I meant, if you want to come over."

"Oh. OK," I said again.

"See ya soon, then?"

"Yeah, I guess. See ya."

I borrowed CJ's new Fair Isle sweater, which she said brought out my dark eyes and hair really well. She French braided my hair for me, which felt so nice on my head I almost fell asleep while she did it. I remember asking her if her mother worked on her hair every morning. She said yes, and I said with my eyes closed that it must be so annoying. I doubt my mother even knows how to French braid. She doesn't have time to fuss with me in the mornings; she has to be at work by seven-thirty.

We stole some lip gloss from Mrs. Hurley's bathroom to give my lips a wet look. When I looked in the mirror at myself with my hair all pulled back like that, I looked a lot like my dad. I didn't have zits on my forehead at that point, so I didn't have to worry about hiding behind my bangs.

It took me a long time to walk all the way to Tommy's, since I didn't have my bike. I walked there slowly, humming a romantic song I was making up, feeling all soft-focus and like I should have a bouquet of flowers or at least white leather gloves, instead of fuzzy mittens. I was nervous but in a good way; even the snow seemed romantic. I imagined a spotlight following me.

When I got there, Tommy was sitting on his front step, making snowballs and chucking them at the mailbox. His aim was decent; there was so much snow caked around the flag, you could barely see it. I made a tight ball, said a little prayer, and let it fly. I hit the mailbox so hard, it wobbled. When I looked at Tommy, he was grinning that grin of his that got me in the first place. "Good shot," he said.

I shrugged, not wanting him to know how nice it felt to hear that. "What happened to the snow fort?" I asked.

"Jonas is reading."

"Oh."

He picked up another handful of snow and asked, "You want to see our tree house?"

"Sure." Following him around the side of the house, I felt like I should say something. "My dad always meant to build us a tree house. There's a whole pile of lumber in our basement."

"Maybe this spring," Tommy suggested.

"He moved to L.A.," I said. He didn't say anything to that. A girl would've said something in a high voice: *Sorry, oh, my gosh, Los Angeles?* I followed silent Tommy to the little cabin in the middle of his yard. "It's not in a tree," I observed.

"That's just what we call it," he said, ducking inside. I stepped in behind him and tried to think of something nice to say, because my mother says when you go to somebody's house, find something to compliment. But before I could say nice walls or something, Tommy asked me, "Did you ever kiss anybody?"

I looked out the window of the cabin toward his house. I couldn't see anybody looking out at us. "Besides family?" I asked.

"No, your grandmother."

"I was just kidding," I said. I didn't want him to think I was a baby or a prude, so in one motion I turned around, grabbed him, and started kissing.

I tried to do it the way CJ and I had been joking about—you know, rocking your head left and right, put your hand in his hair. I wanted to do it right.

I scared him so bad, kissing him like that, he yanked his head back. "Um, want some hot chocolate?" he asked, and before I had a chance to answer, he left the tree house. He practically ran across the yard. I think I was still puckered when he got to his back door.

I walked home, which took an hour. I punched

myself in the stomach the whole way. *Jerk, jerk, foolish jerk.*

I called him to break up as soon as I got in my house, before I even took off my jacket. Jonas answered the phone.

"Can I talk to Tommy?"

"He's sick," Jonas said.

I had actually made him sick. I sat down on the floor, still in my jacket and boots, leaning against the front door.

"Morgan?" Jonas asked.

"Just tell Tommy I don't want to go out with him anymore."

"OK," Jonas said. "See you in school tomorrow." And that was the end of that. I put the box of red-hots in my desk drawer next to the wadded-up thermometer and left it there unopened, to remind myself of the difference between girlfriends and boys. Also to torture myself. Tommy was out of school sick for a few days, but when he came back we barely looked at each other. I'd already told everybody I'd broken up with him because he was such a horn-dog, kissing me so hard out in his tree house.

fifteen

I touched his hair. Oh, jeez, it tortures me just to think of it, and there he is up in front of the class, finishing his Bring Yourself in a Sack, and I still think he's so cute, which I would never admit. I scare myself sometimes, my hand in his hair and my eyes closed, him pulling away and looking all frightened, me smooching away clueless, making him sick.

I don't care if he thinks I'm a slut, kissing him like that. He's so full of himself, he probably thinks I just couldn't resist him. He's got that smirk on, as he pulls a tiny toy dinosaur out of his bag and explains that the *Tyrannosaurus rex* represents him not just because he's so tough, but also because he has been teaching his little cousin about dinosaurs and being a good older cousin is important to him.

I turn to CJ and roll my eyes, thinking I should get her to break up with him, she's much too good for a jerk like Tommy Levit. She's not looking at me, though. I'll write her a note. I'll apologize for being so moody this morning. When she tried to tell me she wasn't really best friends with Zoe, I walked away, telling her Olivia was waiting for me. That had to hurt. Olivia's mother and CJ's are best friends, so CJ's always getting compared to Olivia at home, never quite measuring up, of course. I, of all people, know how that feels—if you ask my mother, I don't measure up to anybody. I am such a bad friend, to shove Olivia Pogostin at CJ, who was only trying to explain that she'd never betray me.

I pick up my pencil and write quickly: *Sorry I'm such a moody mess. Tommy thinks he's so great. Ha! I have to tell you something URGENT Your best friend, Morgan.*

I haven't thought of anything urgent, but there's still a lot of time left; English/social studies is a double period, which is endless. I'll come up with something. I press down to pull the paper off neatly at the perforations, leaving the raggedy part gripped to the spiral wire. I never get caught passing notes. I take my time, carefully. Folding the note slowly, I look across the row at CJ.

She's passing a note to Zoe.

Zoe catches the note, reads it quick, smiles, and touches her friendship ring with her thumb. CJ touches hers, too, then darts her eyes over at me. She frowns, caught. She covers her friendship ring with the other hand, under her desk.

As if I would care or something.

sixteen

The spatula is sticking out of my bag. It's too big. It doesn't fit. It was a stupid thing to choose; it doesn't define who I am. None of this junk does, really. I don't even know if this is the exact spatula I split my brother's head open with. There are a few spatulas in the drawer. Same as that day I chucked it at Ned when he told me about the tooth fairy, I just grabbed one. This spatula could be as distant from any meaning in my life as any random fork in the kitchen. Unless of course I now chuck it at CJ. Which I'm considering. I start to crumple the note I wrote to her, but instead I tap Olivia on the shoulder.

"Cornelia Jane Hurley," says Mrs. Shepard.

Olivia turns around. I hand the note to her as CJ takes a deep breath. Too bad, CJ. You just lost me.

Olivia looks surprised. She's opening the note. I wish I could grab it back from her. I lower my eyes, down to my bag. A stick, I have here, a Barbie head, an eraser, and now I'm passing notes to Miss Perfect saying she's my best friend? When she has all interesting, perfect things in her Sack. I have a twig from the cherry tree. Well, at least I chose one thing that makes sense. This dead twig is totally me.

seventeen

The first day of school this year I stood at my new locker. Me, CJ, Zoe, and Olivia were joking about the puny sixth graders, but really we were sizing one another up. Zoe was tugging at her T-shirt; I think she's embarrassed that her hips grew already. Olivia, who looks like a fourth grader at most, has the locker between me and Zoe, and she was huddled on the floor, organizing it. I looked down at her perfectly straight part, her dark hair tugged tightly to the sides into two pigtail braids. I don't think she grew over the summer at all. She probably stayed inside the whole time diagramming sentences. Her family is best friends with CJ's, and although every mother in Boggs thinks Olivia is the perfect child, Olivia totally worships CJ.

Tommy Levit passed us, yelling, "Wait for you by the wall!"

"They're coming?" I asked Zoe, looking at CJ and shaking my head. Zoe hadn't even asked me and CJ if we minded if the boys joined us, going to get school supplies at Sundries. We had made plans, me and CJ, and we were nice enough to include Zoe. Now the boys were already waiting for us out by the wall.

"If that's OK," Zoe answered, tucking her hair behind her ear.

CJ shrugged slightly. She checked her bun with her wiry, nervous fingers. I could tell she'd go along with whatever I wanted to do.

"Fine," I said. "I don't care if they come."

"Me, too," CJ said, and drooped over gracefully to retie her Keds. She doesn't bend her knees. She got that habit from Fiona the Boring.

Olivia slammed her locker shut and said, "Have fun getting school supplies."

"Have fun at the orthodontist," Zoe answered.

"That's likely," said Olivia. "Hey, you three want to come over, after? We could play pool. I should be done by four-fifteen."

We said sure. Nobody has anything against Olivia; she's always sort of been on the outskirts of our group. She slammed her locker and ran to meet her mother, saying, "Wish me luck!"

"Luck!" Zoe yelled in her booming voice.

CJ whispered, "Olivia's mother told my mother that Olivia thought she might not need braces."

We all shook our heads. Olivia has extremely crooked teeth.

We ambled out into the heat of the afternoon where the Levits were sweating, kicking the wall, waiting for us. Jonas is in chorus with me instead of band with CJ and Zoe and Tommy, so he and I walked ahead, making up nasty lyrics to the ancient cornball chorus songs. I don't know why I don't like Jonas, I started to think—he's a lot easier to talk to than Tommy.

When we got to Sundries and started rummaging through the school supply area, Jonas threw a big gummy eraser in my basket. I threw one in his, too. Then I walked away, quick, over to CJ at the counter. I didn't have enough money to buy more than a couple of things, anyway, and the gummy eraser was a dollar fifteen. I had saved my money all summer, but I was reserving eleven dollars for the Barbie doll whose head is now in my sack. Every time I start to save up, there's something I suddenly get the urge to blow it all on.

CJ was looking at friendship rings in the case, so we picked out the one we both liked. I was relieved she liked a sort of plain one, with just a simple knot in the silver. I'd never want to wear something all gaudy. Not that I could afford to buy it anyway, but still. I hadn't told her about the Barbie I had put on hold, right there under the Sundries front counter. CJ has dozens; she wouldn't understand why I'd waste my own money.

We crossed our fingers and touched our noses. I've really outgrown stuff like that, but CJ hasn't.

After all five of us bought our stuff, we walked down the strip to the pizza place. Jonas slid in next to me on the bench, but I made sure not to look at his cute rosy cheeks too much, because I didn't want him thinking I liked him or something. Tommy spent the whole time telling us about their little cousin, how he taught him all about dinosaurs over Memorial Day weekend.

CJ and Zoe were leaning toward him, nodding and sipping their sodas through straws. All I could think was, *How am I supposed to pay my share of this check? I'm not even supposed to go to the pizza place; we have no money to waste on extravagances.* I held the new gummy eraser in my palms, rolling it between them, under the table. I didn't need it; I mean, pencils have erasers built right in on top for free.

Then Tommy jutted his chin toward me. I didn't know what he'd just said, because I was mentally adding up what change I still had in my pocket, so I just looked away. We had finished the pizza, so it was time to put money on the tray. They probably all think I'm a cheap jerk, but too bad. I only had half a cup of soda and one slice.

Mrs. Levit was waiting outside in her Audi. She waved to us as the boys climbed into the backseat with their school supply bags. Me, CJ, and Zoe walked to Olivia's house to shoot some pool. CJ's ballet classes hadn't started up yet, so she had this one week to hang out.

We chalked up the pool cues and chose sides—me and Olivia against CJ and Zoe. Zoe looked at me like ha, I'm partners with CJ! As if I would care. Just because Olivia is about a decade away from puberty.

We got to talking about boys while we played, or rather while Zoe and Olivia played. CJ and I totally stunk. We were cracking ourselves up. You could see Zoe and Olivia were trying to be good sports, but the worse me and CJ played, the more we laughed, and then we could barely hit the white ball at all. It was funny, how uncoordinated we were, and how NOT seriously we both take pool playing. We were hugging each other, falling down laughing at what LOSERS we were. It was really fun.

But then CJ started acting all cutesy, arabesquing

toward me on her pool cue, asking me which I would kiss if I had to kiss one of the Levits. She was practically announcing she liked Tommy.

"I hate them both," I said.

Zoe said she liked them both but just as friends, and Olivia said she wasn't really friends with any of the boys.

"I just think it was really selfish of them, not to offer us a ride," I said, not getting out of Zoe's way when it was her turn to shoot. Tough.

Olivia accused me of still being mad about the treehouse kiss. I blew that off, joking about how he almost broke my jaw, kissing me. "I just think, common courtesy, they could've offered us a ride."

Zoe and CJ won the pool game. I was happy to be done with it. So boring. We went upstairs to eat ice cream in Olivia's humongous kitchen. There was a round table in the eating area that would take up practically my entire living room, and then in the actual cooking area there was an island and a refrigerator the size of my room, next to a freezer equally huge. The cabinets were wood and glass, the countertops and table gleaming white. My mother would die for a day in there. Someday I'm going to get rich and buy her a house like Olivia's.

"You know what we should do?" I licked the ice cream off my spoon and waited for answers. Nobody came up with one so I said, "We should give the boys S.T.—the Silent Treatment. Teach them a lesson."

CJ was into it right away, so Olivia said fine, too; she'll do anything CJ does. She just kept spooning out the ice cream, saying, "I'm not friends with the boys anyway."

Zoe looked at CJ, like it was CJ's decision.

"Don't do it if you don't want to," I told her. "I just think we girls have to stick together."

"OK," Zoe said. "I'll give them S.T."

I probably would've had more respect for her if she just stuck to her own opinion. All of a sudden CJ is the decision maker of seventh grade?

CJ's mother beeped to pick us up. I'm the only one who thanked Olivia. She seemed sad we were leaving. Her brother, Dex, the hottest eighth grader, came out of the bathroom as we were on our way out their back door. I hadn't realized he was home. I just heard the flush, so I turned toward it, and by accident I looked right into Dex's eyes.

He looked past me and said, "Hi, CJ."

"Hi, Dex," she answered. They're family friends. He doesn't really know me, so I wasn't upset or anything.

In the car, Zoe was chatting with Mrs. Hurley, who looks down on me, so I stared out the window instead of talking to anybody. We dropped Zoe off first. Her pretty Tudor house sits in the crook of the bend on Woodsley Road, so that's where everybody plays flashlight tag on late fall afternoons when it's dark before dinner. Zoe is the fifth of five blond-haired girls, all tall and toothy, athletic, popular, super-friendly. Everybody in Boggs knows the Grandons. Everybody buys their bread and cakes at Grandon Bread, her big bear of a father's bakery, and their cars at her always-smiling-mother's dealership, City Motors, down in Springfield. The Grandons don't lock their back door. Kids are always streaming in and out, and there's always a plate of cookies or brownies cooling on the counter, and nobody gets yelled at for crumbs. They're almost a town joke, the whole family is so perfect. My brother is in eleventh grade with Zoe's sister Bay, and like Zoe, Bay is totally rah-rah, on three varsity teams, including starting singles on the boys' tennis team. Ned went out with Bay when they were in sixth grade, but he has sunk way below her in social standing as he's become weirder and pimplier. In his yearbook for accomplishments, they'll probably list Once Dated Bay Grandon.

Zoe ran around back, waving at us and smiling. I looked the other direction.

When they dropped me off, I unlocked the door and yelled, "Hey, everybody! I'm home!" That's my little joke with myself. Ned works at McDonald's until seven, and Mom goes to school right from work, so she's never home before eight, weekdays.

I sat with the phone on my lap for a few minutes, then dialed my father's California number. When his machine picked up, I was so relieved. "Hello, Dad," I said. "It's Morgan. Listen, can you send me money for new soccer cleats? They're like fifty dollars and Mom is buying my sneakers, when she gets her next paycheck, but seriously, Dad, my feet grew two sizes and all I can fit into is my sandals." I told myself to shut up and quit begging, I sounded so horribly pathetic to myself. "Anyway," I added. "If you can. Call me. OK? 'Bye."

As I was about to hang up, I thought of something to add. "I hope you're out getting your big break!"

I hung up quick. What a stupid thing to say. I sounded like such an imbecile.

I sat there on the couch trying to think of what to do. I decided maybe it would be fun to trash Zoe in my head. A little nastiness sometimes does the trick for me, and Zoe deserved to be my victim du jour, I decided. What a jerk Zoe had been all afternoon, bragging about how close she is with the Levit boys, and acting like she had some inside joke going with CJ when she knew CJ was my best friend.

I decided those thoughts were just too catty to keep to myself, so I dialed CJ's number.

"Hi," I said when she picked up.

"Hi," she said back and waited.

"Well," I said. "That was interesting, wasn't it?"

"What?"

"You don't think she'll give them the Silent Treatment, do you?"

"Who?" CJ asked. "Zoe?"

I lay down on the couch and stared at the ceiling with a pillow on my stomach. "Obviously, Zoe," I said. "She's such good friends with them, all that."

"Yeah," CJ whispered. "But she said she would."

"It'll be hard for her, don't you think? When she starts wanting to be a girl instead of just one of the guys. I mean, they all like her and everything, but she's not the type a boy would ask out or anything. Right?"

"Because she's so friendly?" CJ asked.

"Ned only likes girls who treat him like dirt," I whispered. "And who have really little butts."

CJ sort of giggled, I think.

"Pool was fun, though," I added.

"Yeah," CJ said. "Boy, do we stink! Listen, I have to go stretch. For ballet."

"I gotta go, too," I said. Right. Lots to do. "See you tomorrow. Don't say anything to Zoe."

We hung up. I sort of wished I had homework or something.

I was still lying on the couch staring at the ceiling when Ned came home and dropped a Happy Meal on my lap. He gets an employee discount. Mom came in a half hour later and took a seat next to us on the couch, pulled off her shoes, and leaned back with a sigh to watch TV.

The phone rang while we were flipping from one stupid sitcom to another, and Ned lunged for the phone. Mom raised her eyebrows. "A girl?" she asked. I shrugged. Since Bay Grandon broke up with him, Ned stopped talking about his private life.

"Yeah?" he said into the phone.

"SO cool," Mom whispered, fake-proud.

"Oh. Hello," he said next, through clenched teeth, so I knew he'd heard an Irish accent. I picked up the remote control and raised the volume.

Ned listened for another minute, then held the phone toward me.

I rolled my eyes and grunted, "Hello?"

"Maggie," Dad said. "How's my girl?"

"Fine," I said.

"Listen, about the cleats," he said. I knew already, by the way he said that, what his answer was. "Tough month here in Tinseltown. No work for studs like your old man."

"OK," I said, staring at the TV.

"Hey, but when I hit it big you'll have all the shoes you want."

"Fat lot of good that does me now," I said. "'Bye."

"Let me talk to your mother, hey, Duckie?"

I held the phone out to Mom without moving my eyes from the TV screen.

Mom grabbed the phone and stood up, knocking over the bowl of popcorn. She made an F sound with her mouth but stopped herself. She'd given me and Ned a whole speech earlier in the week about needing to clean up our mouths, all of us—decrease our vocabularies by a few four-letter words.

"Eddie?" she barked into the phone, and it sounded pretty much like the f-word she'd stopped herself from spitting out, the way she said it.

I pretended I was totally engrossed in the commercial on TV, lifting my legs lazily off the coffee table when Ned crawled under them to pick up popcorn kernels and slam them into the bowl.

"No," Mom said, pacing barefoot in tight circles near the dining room table, her fist grasping a clump of her black curly hair. "No, Eddie, you listen to me! Where the . . . No! Where is the check?" Mom glanced over at me, her lips pressed tight against each other, her high cheekbones burning red. She stomped into her room and slammed the door.

"Don't slam doors!" Ned whispered. We grinned

briefly at each other. Then he shrugged. "He's living with that girl, out there, you know. That ditz who dragged him out there."

"No kidding," I answered, totally shocked but trying not to show it.

"I wasn't sure if you knew."

"Of course I knew." I could barely breathe.

"Isn't it gross?" Ned whispered. "He met her at Mass?"

"I know it," I managed to say. I knew he'd been going to seven o'clock Mass every morning, but I was nine, I didn't think anything of it. I just thought, that's what Daddy does. I thought he was holy.

Ned shook his head. "He's such a zip."

"He moved out there with her," I added, not knowing if it were true or not.

"Obviously."

I stared at the TV and said, "I wasn't sure if you knew."

Ned wedged the refilled popcorn bowl next to me on the couch. We used to be buddies, Ned and me, when we were kids—always played together, at least until he got all crazy in seventh grade. People used to say what a perfect family we were.

Ned went into his room and turned on his head-banger music. I turned down the TV volume, so I could eavesdrop on my mother.

I had my ear pressed against the wall when Mom screamed, "AGAIN?"

I slumped back down onto the couch. I knew this one by heart. No check again this month.

"Eddie, what am I supposed to do? You HAVE TO find the money, I don't care if you . . . Too bad, your dream! You're an adult, Eddie, and I bet your little girlfriend doesn't have to . . . What? Do you think I give a rat's . . . I work sixty hours a . . . What? Don't tell me I'm hysterical, you sack of useless . . . What? Yeah? Well, then, get your head out of my teeth, you don't want me biting it off. Yeah? Right back at you."

I heard the phone slam into her door. It's our fourth new phone in a year. I turned the TV volume back up loud, then flung the remote against the bookcase. The battery rolled under the couch. It's our third remote.

I went into my room and closed the door softly, chose a sharp pencil, and took out the small, square, blank book I use as my journal. I wrote down everything that had happened that day, the first day of seventh grade. I wrote and wrote, until I got up to the part about Mom yelling at Dad, and finding out the truth of why Dad had left us. Then I started erasing, with the new gummy eraser. I didn't like it, any of it.

I erased the whole day.

eighteen

The next day, CJ was giving me the Silent Treatment more than the boys. I have no idea why. At our lockers before lunch, CJ even gave her new combination to Zoe instead of to me.

In case CJ gets sick or something, Zoe could unlock her locker and get her stuff for her, and bring it over to her house. I actually live closer to CJ than Zoe does. Last year when CJ got bronchitis, I brought her not just the homework, almost every day, but also, each time, a little thing—a paper-clip bracelet once and the next day a fortune-telling origami thing I spent the entire day making for her. Nothing big. Nothing great. I was the one who had her combination, then.

Zoe's shiny blue eyes opened wide as she looked

down at CJ's new combination for a second before she folded it up and crammed it into her shorts pocket. She smiled her molar-exposing smile at me, almost like she was apologizing. Like I cared or something, that CJ gave her the combination and saved me all that work of making presents and bringing the homework if she gets sick this year.

Zoe could blurt it out to the boys, was the only thing. I wasn't getting the impression she'd been one hundred percent successful at giving them the Silent Treatment, which we had all made a pact to do. CJ could end up with every boy in the school rummaging through her locker, trusting Zoe Grandon, the blabbermouth, with her combination. Zoe had already announced her own locker combination out loud: 7-14-2. Anyone with a locker near ours could steal her lunch or jacket any time. Zoe has no sense of privacy or secrecy.

If CJ hates me, I remember thinking, *What will I do?* I tried to think how to win her back. "Well, my father is at it again," I said.

CJ whispered, "Oh, no," and gave me that head tilted, hand-up-by-her-neck imitation of her mother when she's trying to be sympathetic. At least she still cared. I didn't look away like I usually do when she acts all nice.

"What happened?" Zoe asked.

"You wouldn't understand," I explained to her. "You have the perfect family." I wrote down my new combination and gave it to Olivia. I can give my combination to whoever I want, same as CJ, and Olivia is much more honest and moral than anybody else around; exactly the type of person you'd want to give your combination to. "Here's my combination," I told Olivia.

"Thanks," Olivia said. She couldn't give me her combination because she has a key lock. Everybody else has combinations. Last year I might have thought she was a loser for doing something different, but I am not such a conformist anymore. She can have a key lock if she wants. How generous of me. I watched her lock up, her long, skinny fingers carefully turning the key. She's the least rough person I've ever noticed. Definitely a good person to trust with your combination.

CJ slammed her locker shut.

"My family is so far from perfect," Zoe protested.

I leaned against Olivia's locker and said, "The Grandons? You're all so happy and friendly and cute, we could throw up." In fact, I felt like throwing up.

"Mm-hmm," CJ agreed. "Everybody thinks so." Then she smiled at me. *Thank the Lord*, I thought.

Zoe tugged at her T-shirt and fidgeted around. "My family? Please." She smiled big at CJ.

"Face it, Zoe," I told her. "You have no problems."

She had no answer for that, so she asked what my father had done.

"He called last night with this whole thing, there won't be a check again this month, blah, blah, blah."

Nobody said anything. We started walking to the cafeteria. I could just hear my mother saying, *You sure have a gift for killing a conversation, Morgan.* To lighten things up, I added, "You should've heard my mom. She went nuts. And she says I have a nasty mouth."

CJ put her arm around me. I didn't shrug it off; it felt good even though I had to hunch a little because I grew a few inches this summer.

We sat down at our lunch table. CJ and Olivia were both looking at me all sympathetic as we opened our lunches, so of course Zoe had to horn in on the attention. "My family isn't so perfect," she mumbled.

"Yeah, right," I said.

She was still smiling like she always does, but I noticed for the first time that there was a tightness around her mouth and that her hands were fluttering up near her face nervously. "My sister Colette got her belly button pierced," Zoe said in a quivering voice. "And my dad saw it."

CJ turned away from me to look wide-eyed at Zoe. "Did he have a fit?"

"Oh, yeah," Zoe answered with her mouth full. "When I was on the phone with you?" she said to CJ.

CJ nodded. So I guess they were on the phone together last night. I shoved my uneaten sandwich back into my lunch bag.

Zoe nodded, too, swallowing. "That was my father," she said. "Screaming at Colette that she better have it out by today, and she's screaming no way, it's her body, he can't make her, and he's like, oh, yes, I can. CJ was on the phone with me the whole time."

Hurray for you, I thought.

"That's true," CJ whispered to me and Olivia. "I heard the whole thing."

Olivia opened her pretzel sticks and told Zoe, "I agree with your sister. Even though, gross, still, it's her body." She held the box toward me.

I took a pretzel and, sucking on it, said, "Maybe." They waited while I chewed. I don't talk with my mouth full. "But your sister doesn't have to make such a dramatic point about it."

Zoe shrugged and said, "Well, anyway, my family is far from perfect."

Tommy and Jonas were suddenly sitting down at our table. I hadn't even seen them walk over. As they climbed onto the bench, CJ was telling Zoe, "You must be so upset."

"Why?" Tommy asked. "What happened?" He pointed his chin at me, as if I would be the one to break our Silent Treatment and explain.

"Nothing," I said.

CJ put her arm around Zoe. Jonas reached across me and grabbed a couple of Olivia's pretzel sticks. *Excuse me, am I invisible?*

"You could ask," I told him.

He stopped chewing and lowered the uneaten halves of the pretzel sticks back into Olivia's box. "Sorry," he mumbled, and stood up.

"Later," Tommy said as they walked away in their untied high-tops.

"Much," Zoe said.

That made me laugh. She really is funny, I thought. So I asked her if her father is actually going to check her sister's belly button. She nodded with a nauseated look on her face and said, "Tonight." She tried to smile and added, "Should be a comedy."

CJ, who knows nothing about families falling apart, told Zoe, "If you need to get away, you can call me and come over."

"Or me," I offered. "Anytime."

CJ smiled at me.

Olivia told Zoe, "My house is closest. You can ride your bike over if you want."

Zoe told the three of us that we're the greatest. Then the Levit boys threw a bunch of minimarsh-mallows at us. We laughed and gobbled them up.

After school, I rode straight to Sundries instead of home. My money was in my pocket, and I plunked it on the counter as soon as I walked in and checked that nobody I knew was in the store.

"Wait a while," said slow Mrs. Dodge, who owns the place. "Catch your breath."

I hate when old people feel like they can tell kids what to do. I looked at the ceiling and waited, count-ing silently to ten. "May I please have the thing?"

"What thing?"

"That I put on hold," I whispered. "The Barbie."

"Ah," she said in a voice so loud it echoed through-out the store. "The doll. Yes." She bent down to re-trieve it from under the counter. I prayed she'd hurry, because I could just imagine each person I knew strolling in right then—Zoe. Tommy. My brother.

Mrs. Dodge turned the Barbie box over and over in her hands.

"Ten ninety-eight," I finally said, though I knew rushing her was totally counterproductive.

"Is it?" She studied the box. "Ah, there it is. Plus tax, of course. Funny, usually the younger girls go for these things. Don't see the appeal, myself."

I forced myself to stifle the comments and just subtly push the stack of carefully saved dollars across the counter, another inch closer to her. She rang up the sale on her cash register and slipped the box into a white paper bag. I grabbed the bag out of her hand and almost left without my change.

Instead of crushing Barbie in my rattrap, I rode home one-handed, peeking into the bag as I rode. *Mine*, I thought. *Finally.*

Mine didn't come with a fancy outfit or even a decent pair of pumps, just a cheap-looking hot-pink minidress and matching hot-pink sneakers in a plastic bag taped inside the box. But the others, the Barbies in the better clothes, were twice as expensive, and it had taken so long to save up for this one I just couldn't wait anymore. I was so excited, I could barely wait to get home and yank her out. She was tied to the box with a bunch of Baggie ties and a plastic tab anchored in her head. I used a scissors on that. It was quite a project, getting her free. Her hair was sewn to the box under a plastic piece. I was scared I might ruin her. I searched for Barbie removal instructions, but there weren't any—just small print on the bottom back panel that said DOLLS CANNOT STAND ALONE.

Oh, well, I thought. *I don't care if she stands alone. She'll be hiding under my bed her whole life anyway.* But only if I could get her hair off the box. How does anybody else know how to do it? Why in the world would they sew her hair between a plastic piece and the box? It seems so gruesome.

I guess a mother would normally handle the Barbie removal. A mother would know how, but mine wasn't due home for a few hours and anyway she'd outlawed Barbies years before. I was on my own.

I closed my eyes and pulled. My jaw was gripped tight with all the force it took to tear that plastic thing away from the cardboard it was sewn to. When I opened my eyes, though, she was free. And only slightly mussed.

I didn't care that she'd be a minor Barbie to anybody else. She's my first one, my only one. Anyway I'm too old to play with Barbies. I smoothed her hair down and whispered, "Hi. I'm Morgan."

I felt completely idiotic. I held her up and looked her over. "Your outfit is tacky, but I love you, and I'll take care of you," I whispered. I felt myself start to cry a little. What a sap.

I sat there in my room trying to figure out how to play with my Barbie for a while. I moved all her movable parts, but without a change of clothes or any accessories, there just aren't many activity options.

I called CJ. I didn't really have anything to say. "Hi," I said, looking at my new Barbie, so beautiful.

"Hi," she said back.

I wanted to tell her, but I didn't want her to think I was a big fool. "You want to do the math homework?" I asked her instead.

"Sure," CJ whispered.

I laid Barbie on my pillow and picked up my math text. Math isn't easy for CJ. I guess a lot of girls don't like it, but I love math. Not that I'd ever say so. But it's like puzzles to solve. I pretended, over the phone, to be having more trouble with it than I was, staring down at the answer already on my paper. "I don't know," I said. "Wait, do we subtract that?" It felt good to hear CJ laugh with relief. "What a couple of losers," I said. She laughs like huh, huh—very breathy. She used to stutter, so now she doesn't say much and what she says, she whispers.

"Did my hair look terrible today?" she whispered.

"What?" I asked, stalling. She always wears it pulled back in a tight bun, but that day she'd worn it down, or rather, out. She has very curly hair, which she brushes after it's dry so it poofs up around her tiny face. It honestly isn't the most attractive thing. If I were her I'd at least use a barrette, but she goes to extremes—bun or frizz.

"It looked gross, didn't it?" she asked.

"No," I lied. Did she want the truth or nice? "You know, I have a barrette that would look good on you."

"I, no, that's, I'm never wearing it down again," she said. "I gotta go."

"Nobody noticed it anyway," I assured her. "'Bye."

I picked up Barbie and lifted her dress. No belly button. If I got my belly button pierced nobody would even notice. But still, you have to feel bad for somebody who looked as sad and tense as Zoe did at lunch. CJ is not the only one who can act sympathetic, I decided. I dropped Barbie on my desk blotter, looked up Zoe's number in my address book, and dialed her number. *I'm not selfish*, I congratulated myself as I waited for an answer.

"CJ?" Zoe asked as soon as she picked up.

"Zoe?" I asked.

"Morgan?" Zoe asked back.

"Yeah." I picked up my Barbie and went out back to the deck to sit on the rocking chair. "Were you expecting CJ?" Did they have plans to talk to each other? I started feeling very paranoid.

"No," Zoe stammered. "I just, what's up?"

I blew my long bangs out of my eyes and squinted into the setting sun. Ned and Mom wouldn't be home for a few hours, so it was safe to have my Barbie out. I bent her stiff creaky knees and tried to give her a little hug. She wasn't at all cuddly.

"Um . . ." I said into the phone. I'd forgotten why

I'd called Zoe. She waited for me to say something. I'd never called her before. What a bonehead, to call her out of the blue, the most popular girl in seventh grade. Who did I think I was? "I was just wondering," I said, trying to think of something. "Did you get the math homework? I, um, forgot to write it down."

"Oh, sure!" She ran and got the assignment, and I pretended to do it all over again with her. My mind had plenty of time to wander. I was wondering where Zoe was sitting while we talked, if she was on her back porch, too, and if so, could she see the Levit boys? What if they were in their "tree house"? Which of course got me remembering being in there with Tommy last year, mashing my face against his, and how good it felt at the time, and how awful, after.

Without realizing it I blurted out, in the middle of a word problem, "Do you think we were overly harsh on the boys today?"

"I don't know," she answered. I knew she hadn't wanted to ignore them; I knew she was friends with them, easy with them in a way I can't figure out how to be. She just goes off and plays catch with them if she feels like playing catch, even if she's the only girl. She's the least self-conscious person I know. If I weren't best friends with CJ, I realized, maybe I'd be best friends with Zoe. Not that she would want to be, with me. Obviously.

"They seemed really upset," I told her. I didn't want her to think I never notice another person's feelings.

She agreed that they seemed hurt. We decided we'd end the Silent Treatment. I was relieved. It felt like Zoe and I were getting close, bonding. Like we could really trust each other. So I whispered, "Their haircuts look sort of cute—don't you think?" I curled up my feet underneath me, to warm them. The breeze was picking up as the sun set.

"I didn't notice," Zoe said.

"Oh," I answered, feeling like such a fool. *Such a sex-crazed lunatic*, she must be thinking. *Yuck, who'd want to be friends with Morgan, what a slut.* I changed the subject quick. "Did your dad check Colette yet?"

"No," Zoe said. "Thursday is his late night at the bakery. But she still has it in there, she showed me."

"Are you a wreck?" I asked her in my most sympathetic way. I even held my hand over my heart, the way CJ and her mother do.

"Yeah," Zoe admitted, her voice shaking. I tried to think what CJ would say. She's much nicer than I am, she'd say the right thing. I prayed: *Saint Christopher, please let me say the right thing, I want to say something nice to her.*

Before I could think of something, Zoe asked me how was gym.

We chatted about how stupid gym is, how cloddish

we all feel, especially next to CJ, who can rest her head in the middle of a side split. Zoe told me this fact, like I didn't know my own best friend can rest her head in the middle of her split. I tried not to let that annoy me. If I took ballet four times a week, I'd be able to rest my head in the middle of a split, also. I made my Barbie do a split and raise her arms in the middle—*ta-da!*

We got into the topic of sports, which was sort of a relief. Zoe and I are both pretty competitive. We talked about soccer and then about softball. Our team almost made regionals last year, me at first base and Zoe pitching. We talked about the final game last year, where Zoe made eight strikeouts. I asked, "What did you strike out in that game, seven?"

I wanted to see if she'd correct me. I'm so bad.

"I don't remember," she answered. "Maybe six."

That made me really like her. I know she probably remembered every single pitch but just didn't want to boast. Self-praise stinks, my mother says. As the sun sank below the woods behind the backyard, I hugged my knees for warmth but didn't feel like going inside. The air smelled a little leafy, like fall—like I shouldn't be sitting outside at night in shorts anymore. But, too bad. I felt on the verge of being liked by her. The balance seemed fragile, though; I didn't want to move and risk wrecking it. "What a game that was, huh?" I asked Zoe.

"Yeah," she agreed.

"That ugly girl I thought was gonna cry." The superstar from the other team, this incredibly homely girl, wanted to whack a homer off Zoe so bad, but she'd only been able to tip Zoe's curveball and I raced in and caught it for the final out. I screamed, then charged up and hugged Zoe after, up on the mound. Our sweaty cheeks touched.

She was remembering, too, I bet. She told me I was great at First. I could picture the scene so clearly, our teammates running in from the outfield slapping me and Zoe on the butts with their mitts. We had really dominated, and that team was supposed to be so great. I could still see CJ scrambling slowly in from right field on her skinny legs, being careful not to trip on any divots. She was the last one into the crush of us.

"Just between us," I whispered to Zoe. "Maybe it's good CJ has dance four times a week this year. I mean, no offense," I quickly added. "She's my best friend, but . . ."

"I know," Zoe whispered back. "She has no arm."

I pictured CJ onstage, like when we'd all gone on the class trip last year to see her in *The Nutcracker,* how raging jealous I'd felt, slumped in my velour seat bundled up in a sweater and my corduroys, watching her arms lift so gracefully into the air, her long, thin legs raised strong on *pointe* so beautiful, and then after, riding clenched in my bus seat listening to everybody talk about how special my best friend was, what a star. A better person would've been happy for her but not bitter nasty me.

It felt good, on the phone with Zoe, to realize—I'm better than CJ at something. Maybe it's not so terrible to feel that way, even if it is a little self-praise. CJ's mother always says you have to be dedicated to one thing if you ever want to be good at it. And me and Zoe, we were focusing on sports. So it's only natural we should be better than CJ.

I could feel Zoe's smile, through the phone. She has the best smile of anyone I know, so pure. We promised each other not to say anything to CJ, and agreed to get together for a catch some afternoon. By the time we hung up, it was dark out and really cold. I went inside to boil some hot dogs for my dinner.

While I was eating them, with Barbie sitting on the table keeping me company, CJ called back. She asked if I'd spoken to Zoe.

"No," I lied, before I could stop myself. No reason, just, it sounded like CJ was accusing me. And it had been so nice talking to Zoe, so real and relaxed—I don't know. I guess I sort of wanted to keep it private, not have to tell CJ everything we said. I think you should be able to be best friends and not tell every detail to each other. Also, I didn't want to make her mad. CJ gets mad pretty easy; she's very sensitive. "Why did you ask me that?" I asked her.

"Just wondering," she said in her quiet, slow way.

I was so nervous I started babbling about Zoe, how I like her, to let CJ know I am nice and friendly. I took Barbie's dress off while I talked and her sneakers. When Barbie was naked except for her built-on panties, I told myself to shut up about Zoe already, so I said, "Anyway."

"Yeah?" CJ asked.

Uh-oh, I thought, *maybe CJ is scared I'm choosing Zoe instead of her. Maybe Cornelia Jane Hurley is jealous of me, of all things. If only.*

To make sure CJ knew where my loyalties lay, I knew I had to say something bad about Zoe. So I said something like, *But all Zoe ever talks about is sports.* I said it really critically, so she'd be sure Zoe wasn't suddenly my favorite person. That's the kind of friend I am.

CJ didn't say anything then, which made me even more nervous. I ran my fingers over my pimply forehead. More gravelly than ever. I went to the bathroom to look at it and torture myself, compare myself to Barbie, who hung upside down naked in my fist.

With a headband holding back my long curtain of bangs, I stared at myself and Barbie, side by side in the mirror. "I guess I just feel bad for Zoe," I told CJ. "About the boy thing. You know, like we were saying last night." I thought maybe if I sounded sympathetic, CJ would like that. She always says I should try to be sympathetic. Barbie was smiling encouragement.

"Morgan," CJ whispered.

I plopped Barbie into the sink and leaned toward the mirror to try to pop one of the bigger pimples. Spots, my father calls them. *Can't you get anything to cover those spots?* he'd asked me this summer, on his one quick visit. I've grown my bangs since then, because no medicine or popping seems to be working, and I don't want anybody else looking as grossed out as Dad did. Zoe has the clearest skin; it's perfect, like Barbie's.

CJ whispered, "I didn't say anything about Zoe."

"You know," I reminded her, balancing the phone with my shoulder. "What we were saying last night, about boys liking Zoe but not in *that way.*" Popped one. I grabbed a piece of toilet paper and pressed it against my head. So what? CJ has very sensitive skin, red and blotchy. And Zoe has a big rear end. Barbie can't even stand up. DOLLS CANNOT STAND ALONE, it said right on her box, so I don't know why she thinks she's so perfect. I'm not the only one with flaws. Everybody shouldn't be so judgmental.

"I didn't say that," CJ protested. "I don't know who the boys like."

"Well . . ." She was right, of course. She would never say something nasty about anybody. But I wasn't trying to be mean, either. CJ had sort of agreed, too. I think she did. Why was she twisting it around? The point wasn't that I know who the boys like, anyway.

I could hear her breathing. Not saying anything to me.

I sat down on the closed toilet seat, my head hanging down between my knees. I really didn't feel like beating up on poor Zoe who was sitting alone, probably, waiting for her father to come home and scream like my father used to. But why was CJ being so defensive of her? *Zoe thinks you have no arm*, I wanted to yell. I couldn't, obviously.

"Come on," I tried pathetically. "You know who the boys *don't* like."

"No," CJ whispered. I could hear how angry I was making her but I didn't know how to turn it back to good. I squeezed my head between my knees to keep from puking up the two hot dogs I'd just downed. So much for a good night. What did she want from me? But I refused to cry. If she hates me, well, fine. I inhaled the cold smell of the porcelain of the toilet beneath me. Fine. Be mad at me. Nothing I can do.

CJ mumbled something about having to go.

"Fine," I said, grabbing Barbie out of the sink by her hair. Fine, go be best friends with Zoe if you want, if you feel so defensive of her. I don't care. Nobody stays around me long anyway, and I don't blame any of you. I'm stuck with myself, and I can't say I'm thrilled with the company, either.

I scooped Barbie's tiny pile of clothes off the table on my way into my room and threw them in my garbage. I sat down on my bed, crossed my legs, and looked at Barbie. *I wanted you for so long,* I told her. *I saved and saved to buy you. But now that I have you I'm too old to play with you. You're no use to me, you stiff-legged-plastic-can't-hug-you, you cannot-stand-alone piece of crap.* I pulled and yanked at her head until it popped off. Underneath was a white plastic thing that looked like a droopy capital T. I looked at the head. Still smiling, of course, hair still perfect. I fished her clothes out of the trash and dressed the body again, carefully.

nineteen

I peek inside my bag, now, at the Barbie head I chose to include as a representation of myself. I can't remember anymore what I meant for it to symbolize.

She's still pretty, though, I think, touching her silky blond hair that had been sewn onto the cardboard of the package. I still like her, as horrible as she is, just a popped-off plastic head.

Mrs. Shepard repeats, "Cornelia Jane Hurley?"

Nobody calls CJ "Cornelia Jane." It's a family name—all the first girls for generations have been named Cornelia Jane, and then they're called by nicknames: Mrs. Hurley is called Corey, and CJ's grandmother is Nellie. Great-grandmother was Lia. Somebody way back a hundred years ago was called just Jane. I know

CJ's whole family history, I've seen all their photo albums. I even know where the photo albums are—in the bottom living room cabinet. CJ and Morgan, Morgan and CJ.

She's still sitting there not moving. I know inside she's not thinking any words, just cringing at the mention of that full big heinous name. If it were me, I might tell Mrs. Shepard to call me CJ, but CJ won't. She won't say anything. She's standing up slowly. I knew it, nothing, not a word. We know everything about each other.

Totally pointless, getting to know every detail about a person if the person could just come in one day wearing a friendship ring with somebody else. I can just forget where the Hurleys keep the photo albums now, and the extra rolls of toilet paper, and the batteries. All the cow accessories in their kitchen.

Olivia flips a note back onto my desk. I cover it with my palm and check Mrs. Shepard. She's looking at the clock. I quietly unfold Olivia's note. It's my note back again, signed "your best friend" and everything. Underneath that Olivia has written, in her perfect script, *Want to come over after school today?*

I don't have the energy to make a new best friend, I decide. I don't want to learn where the Pogostins keep their batteries and what you're not allowed to touch in their living room. I crumple the note softly and shove it into my desk, next to the envelope with the thermometer inside.

I rest my heavy head on my palm, watching CJ make her slow toe-pointing way up to the front of the room.

twenty

This morning I sat on the wall with CJ before school, chatting away about boys and whether I should pull my hair back. I even—oh, shoot me—I even complimented her new ring. What a loser. I was surprised she'd gotten it already, but instead of thinking why would she buy our friendship ring without waiting for me to get the matching one with her, which I just assumed she was planning, I was all worried about how was I going to save up enough to buy mine? Mine. Like it was automatic.

And then Zoe got off the bus, practically waving her matching ring in my face.

"So," CJ asked Zoe. "Did you say anything to Jonas?" CJ's arms were folded, as if she could keep me from noticing her ring after the fact.

"Like what?" Zoe asked her. She hiked her backpack up on her shoulder and played with her ring again. "I mean, they're at my bus stop."

"No," CJ whispered. "About Morgan."

Zoe looked at me and so did CJ. I stared down at my sandals.

"Oh," Zoe said. "Not yet. But listen, Morgan—my sister said yes, you can have her old cleats, for soccer. Size five, right?"

"Yeah," I said, so ashamed I'd had to ask her, hating my father and my mother and everybody, everything.

The warning bell rang.

"I'll bring them in tomorrow," Zoe said.

I shrugged. What did I care about cleats? My best friend just dumped me.

"You'll ask Jonas?" CJ asked Zoe.

Zoe said, "Sure."

"Don't," I told her.

"What?" Zoe asked. "You changed your mind already?" She smiled at me. I wanted to spit. I closed my eyes, thinking, *I have nobody.*

Kids were passing us going in to school.

"You coming?" Olivia asked, stopping to wait for us.

"Zoe?" CJ asked. "Could you grab mine and Morgan's bags? We're too short."

I grabbed my bag. "I can get my own," I said.

Zoe pulled CJ's bag down. "I'll try to talk to Jonas today," she told me.

"No," I said. "I hate him. He walks like a chicken. Ew." I caught up with Olivia and linked my arm into hers, whispering, "Come on, let's go in."

twenty-one

CJ turns carefully, now, as if she might break her body if she moves it abruptly. There is nothing CJ hates so much as speaking in front of the class. In kindergarten she barely said a word. In first grade she never managed to get her full two letters out—all she managed was the first sound, Se-se-se, over and over. My heart hurt for her every time she was asked her name. In fourth grade, after we were best friends already, she told me that she'd rather write a ten-page book report than say her name in front of the class once. When we were partners for a science project last year, I did all the talking so she wouldn't have to, and I also did half the research, but I didn't care if we split the work evenly. I've just always tried to be there for her, to be strong for her, help her stand up for herself whether it's on the playground or to her mother, who totally intimidates her and runs her life. I'd do anything for her; she knows that. Oh, well. Anyway.

CJ takes a big breath of air, the way she learned in speech class. She reaches into her bag and pulls out a toe shoe. Surprise, surprise. "I, I dance," she whispers. Mrs. Shepard says nothing. I touch the ballet slipper in my bag. It's small, left from fourth grade when I had such tiny feet. I never got on *pointe*, so I don't have a toe shoe.

The toe shoe in CJ's shaking hand has faded brown satin peeling off from the toe area; they spray-painted her toe shoes brown last year when she played a bug in *A Midsummer Night's Dream*. She was so good. I went to two performances, even though I had to beg Ned for money for the second ticket and clean his room for the month of February to pay him back. It was worth it. I brought CJ flowers I'd made out of tissues. I sat beside her parents in the orchestra, getting sick off the smell of the beautiful pink roses in her mother's lap through the whole performance. Afterward, we went backstage, and I stood with my green down jacket hanging off my shoulders and my work boots spread in second position, as all the little bunheads buzzed around me in their sheer pale pinks. CJ smiled so happy when she saw me, her cheeks flushed and her eyes sparkling. She was still out of breath, pulling on her leg warmers and her tight little sweater top. The Hurleys invited me out to dinner with them. In the car on the way to the restaurant, I dropped the tissue flowers in CJ's lap and said, "These are stupid, but . . ." She whispered to me that they were way better than the live flowers from her mother, because they'd last forever. She even brought them into the restaurant with us and left the roses out in the car.

Maybe one of those flowers is in her Sack. I see something pink in there, something that looks tissuey.

Please, Saint Christopher, let it be one of my flowers.

I dig into my Sack, looking for the Saint Christopher medal I stole from my father. There it is, sunk down at the bottom. I grab it, hold it between my palms, close my eyes, and pray.

Please, Saint Christopher, please let that be one of the flowers I made for her, let her have chosen something to do with me in her Sack.

She pulls out History, the stuffed dog she got for quitting sucking her thumb when she was two and a half. I almost expect her to tell the story: She stopped sucking her thumb, and as a prize her mother bought her this incredibly snuggly little dog, and suggested they call it Doggie, but CJ, in a rare moment of self-assertion, said, "No, his name is History." I love that story. It's so easy to imagine her all serious as a toddler, shocking everybody by her unexpected strength. People who don't know her so well don't realize that inside all her shy sweetness, there's something tough as steel. I bet her new boyfriend, Tommy, doesn't know it, and neither does her new best friend. I bet they don't even know History's name.

"This is, was, um," CJ starts, and I grip the Saint Christopher medal to pray for her. "This, this, this, dog . . ."

I stop myself from running up to the front of the class and doing her presentation for her. It kills me to see her gulping air, struggling up there. I'm sure I could explain everything in her Sack. I wrap my feet around my chair's legs to keep me planted.

"This is, was, when I was, was a baby, I had this," she almost whispers, and drops History on Mrs. Shepard's desk. She closes her eyes. I close mine.

Please, Saint Christopher, if you let there be something to do with me in CJ's Sack, I'll do anything. I'll change. I'll be nice about CJ choosing Zoe over me. I'll get up in front of the class when it's my turn and admit all this truth about myself. Anything.

I open my hands and look at the medal clutched between them. *I swear it, Saint Christopher—do this one thing for me, and I'll change.*

CJ has one more item to present. I hold the medal and pray.

twenty-two

Exercise bands. "For ballet," CJ says. The same thing she said about the net that holds her bun together during performances, the same thing she said about the pink tissue-y wrap skirt I had stupidly thought might be a crappy fake flower she probably tossed a long time ago. I would've. You don't need old tissues looped with a Baggie tie gathering dust in your room.

She lifts each thing soundlessly off the desk and places it back inside her bag without raising her eyes to us or Mrs. Shepard. I drop the Saint Christopher medal back inside my Sack. I never believed in him anyway. All that is just superstition.

A noise startles me. I turn around to see Zoe Grandon clapping for CJ, breaking the silence in the room by applauding. She doesn't even care that nobody else is joining in, she just claps and claps, her big goofy grin showing every white tooth in her mouth. "Awesome," she says.

I turn to see how CJ is reacting. Her head is bowed but under those thick brown eyebrows, CJ's eyes peer toward the back of the room, and a slow, small grin fights its way onto CJ's serious pale face. She raises her chin and smiles at Zoe.

"Woo!" Zoe yells, pumping her fist in the air.

CJ smoothes her hair back from her face and, smiling at Zoe, walks back to her chair. She turns in my direction but then right past me and whispers thanks to Zoe.

My hand is in the air. "Can I go to the bathroom?"

I stand up and head to the door, clutching my Sack. I can't wait for an answer, I have to go, have to get out. Mrs. Shepard says something about leave my Sack. *You don't need to bring it, do you?*

But I am already out the door and I hear people laughing at me, behind my back, but I gotta go, gotta get out and I don't care, laugh at me if you want. I hear Mrs. Shepard call Zoe Grandon to present next, but that's the last thing I hear, because I round the corner and start to run.

Bathroom. Or nurse. Maybe get sent home, but Mom would have to leave work to pick me up and she'd be all annoyed and who needs it? And I'm not sitting there getting my temperature taken by the nurse like she's doing me a favor. I don't want any favors, I don't want anyone.

It's so pointless. I shuffle as fast as I can down the stairs to the first floor, just moving, just getting away. Pointless. You get attached and they leave, they dump you and there is nothing you can do, chump, nothing. That's what I should have in this Sack. Nothing. I should just throw all this junk in the trash where it belongs and go up and present my nothing. Nothing and nothing and nothing. And if you don't think that's an accurate representation of me in all my various aspects, Mrs. Shepard, well, that's because you have no clue who I am.

I slam my fist into the door of the girls' room, then lean the weight of my body against it to get in. There's a silver trash can in the corner near the sink, and I cross the room in two steps. My Sack is upside down. "Out!" I say out loud. "Get out! I don't want you! I don't need any of this crap, just a bunch of garbage I've been hoarding as if it means something to anybody. Get out!"

The branch is stuck. "Get! Garbage, that's where you belong, you worthless . . ."

I shove, but it's caught on the lid. I can't even throw away trash. "Get in there you stupid fruitless—never grew a single pitiful cherry, you stupid, get in!"

I yank the branch out to put it in straight. My finger touches something sticky. I look down to see what disgusting thing is now all over my thumb, is it bird poop or what, so typical it figures. What is this thing, black and sticky?

Oh. Tape.

I close my eyes and sit down on the cold green bathroom tile, next to the garbage can full of my stuff. I touch the sticky spot on the branch in my hand, remembering Mom's face when she was looking out the kitchen window, staring at the cherry tree.

It didn't last, obviously, but for a minute she was happy. She believed, for that minute, that my tree wasn't defective, that it had really managed to burst out in a thousand cherries. It was just a trick, not magic. I know, obviously, since I'm the faker, I'm the one who did the tricking. The only thing is, for a minute she believed, and that minute felt like magic to me. Real magic.

Too bad if she thought it was stupid and a waste of money. It was worth eighteen dollars, seeing her so happy she was shaking as she stood there pointing out the window. She thought she was witnessing a miracle. I made that happen. And it was my eighteen dollars, so screw her. Best eighteen dollars I ever spent.

I push myself off the bathroom floor.

twenty-three

The sealed box of red-hots.
The little white box with my baby tooth in it.
The spatula.
The gummy eraser, its corner used up.
The pale pink ballet slipper.
The Barbie head, still pleasantly smiling.
The medal of Saint Christopher, hanging from the chain.

All fifty-two cards, bound again with the rubber band and wiped clean from the gook at the bottom of the garbage can.

The branch from the cherry tree that did get cherries, and they were real, and my mother felt lucky to have them, at least for a minute. Maybe other people would think it's stupid or pathetic, but it's mine, this branch—like all the rest of the stuff I'm picking out of the trash and loading again into this brown bag. It means something to me.

twenty-four

Head down, I walk as quickly and quietly as I can up the aisle to my seat. Zoe is just finishing her presentation. "And, here's the tenth thing: my shoelace." She pulls a gray shoelace out of her bag.

Mrs. Shepard asks, "A shoelace?"

"Yes, because"—Zoe touches the frayed tip of the shoelace—"because I'm just barely holding myself together!" Everybody laughs, including me. I can't help it. Even though she stole my best friend, she really is funny, and her smile is so broad. She looks at me. I try to decide what to do—smile back? Or let her know she can't win me over so easy? Not after what she's done. I stop smiling and just stare. She blinks a few times, then says, "Well, that's me! In a nutshell. In a Sack. That's it."

"Fine," Mrs. Shepard says.

Zoe shrugs and starts tossing her things back in her Sack. Even though I do have to hate her, I sort of wish I hadn't missed her presentation. People are leaning back in their chairs like they just ate something good, watching her. I think she just put a piece of French toast in a Baggie into her Sack. What could that have meant?

I clutch the wrinkled brown bag on my lap. *My stuff*, I remind myself. *Maybe it's not as good as Zoe's or Olivia's or CJ's, but what can I do? You play the hand you're dealt, as Mom would say.*

Zoe is walking up the aisle toward me and CJ. CJ smiles at her, clapping a little with her hands down by the edge of her desk. I look away, into my desk.

There's the crumpled note from Olivia. I smooth it out. As Zoe passes me, I'm reading it again.

Sorry I'm such a moody mess. Tommy thinks he's so great. Ha! I have to tell you something URGENT. Your best friend, Morgan.

And then under that, in Olivia's perfect script, *Want to come over after school today?*

I pick up my pen and write, in script, *Yes.*

Zoe sits down in her seat.

I fold the note carefully into a little square and grip it in my palm, rubbing my thumb over it, deciding.

twenty-five

"Morgan Miller."

Clutching my bag, I walk up to the front of the room. On my way, I secretly drop the note on Olivia's desk. Her thin hand darts out to cover it.

At the front, I turn and face the class. I don't want to look at anybody. Taking my cue from Olivia, I look straight at the bulletin board behind and above their heads. "So," I say. "This is me."

I pull the spatula out of the bag. "A spatula." I swallow. "Because, um, my hobby is cooking." I glance at CJ, who is squinting. She knows I don't cook. I look back at the bulletin board and add, "Also, I once flung it at my brother and cut his head open."

Somebody laughs, I'm not sure who. I smile and reach back into my bag. "This is a ballet slipper." As I'm holding it up for the class to see, the Saint

Christopher medal falls out of it, onto the floor. "Oops." I pick it up. Now I've got the ballet slipper in one hand and the Saint Christopher medal in the other. "And this is a, it used to belong to my, it's a religious thing, medal, because, thank God, I don't have to dance ballet anymore. Ha, ha, ha."

I set them both down on Mrs. Shepard's desk.

"Here's a deck of cards," I say, pulling them out of my Sack. "They belong to my mother, and she taught me how to play gin, and I really like doing that. You know, sometimes. Because sometimes I beat her."

I'm about to put them down, but then I think of something to add. "Also, my mother always used to say, 'You play the hand you're dealt,' which means, I think, that, you know, you get what you get, so you may as well try to win with what you've got, and that's like, my philosophy in life. I think. Maybe."

I wish I hadn't said that. It sounded better inside my head. I look into the bag quick for something less personal, but the hard thing is all my stuff is really personal. I choose the Barbie head, and pull her out by the hair.

Swinging her back and forth upside down, I explain, "My mother didn't want me to have Barbies when I was little, because they repress girls' ambitions, or something like that."

I think Mrs. Shepard just nodded, but I'm not sure.

"Well, I wanted one anyway, so I bought this one, and it didn't do anything bad to me. It just, didn't do much at all. So I popped her head off."

I swing Barbie's head onto the ballet slipper.

"What else," I mumble, peering inside my bag. "Oh, this is a branch from my cherry tree. My parents planted it the day I was born." I stand in front of them, touching the sticky spot, thinking how to explain.

I shrug and place it beside the Saint Christopher medal.

Looking inside the Sack, I take a deep breath and tell myself, *Get it over with, fast.* I pull out the red-hots and say, "This is for my sweet tooth." I drop the box on the desk so quick it falls right off, crashes onto the floor, and pops open. Red-hots scatter everywhere. I feel my cheeks getting hot, and the tears welling up behind my eyes, but no way I'm going to fall apart. "Well, so much for that," I say, trying to smile.

"Finish," Mrs. Shepard says. "You can sweep at the end of class."

"OK, sorry," I mumble.

I don't want to look at her or anybody. Almost done, almost done, just survive it. I pull out the eraser. "I make a lot of mistakes," I say. "Obviously."

I think Mrs. Shepard smiled.

It gives me courage to look at the faces in front of me. Nobody is sneering or grimacing. Zoe is nodding, actually. Jonas has his head tilted sideways, like he's really listening, and although Tommy is chewing on his thumbnail, he's looking right at me. Olivia is leaning forward, her face in her hands, smiling. I avoid looking at CJ. I'm just not ready. I place the eraser beside the branch and go back to the bag.

The tooth jiggles inside the small white box as I lift it. I open the box. "This is the first baby tooth I lost. Because, it's to symbolize, you know . . ." I close my eyes. Say something. "It's for like, getting rid of the baby parts of me."

I open my eyes and look right at Mrs. Shepard. "That's it." I shrug.

"That's nine things," she says.

"Nine?" I start counting, but before I hit five I realize, *Oh, no—the thermometer is in my desk.* "Oh," I say while my mind is going warp speed. Do I go get it? How do I explain a broken thermometer without starting to cry, without looking straight at CJ and in front of all these people saying, *You are part of me, why don't you want me anymore? How can you replace me so easily?*

Obviously I will never embarrass myself like that. What, then? Somebody shifts, I hear the bottom of a chair squeal against the floor. Mrs. Shepard taps her toe. Once, twice.

"Because," I say, thinking, *Because what? Because what?* "Because my tenth thing is . . ." *Is what?* This is a nightmare. "My tenth thing . . ." I look into my empty bag as if something might magically materialize. Nothing.

"My tenth thing is nothing."

"Excuse me?" asks Mrs. Shepard.

"It's nothing," I repeat, wondering where I'm going with this. "Not nothing like, poor me, I'm a nothing. That's not what I mean. No, nothing like, the empty bag, because, the most important thing is, about me, is . . ." I'm talking so fast I have to suck in some air quick. "What I mean is, the future. You know, that I'm not done yet, the most important part of me, or the best part, maybe, is what hasn't happened yet. What I haven't made happen yet."

Nobody moves.

"It's hard to explain," I say, loading my things back into the brown paper bag.

"No," says Mrs. Shepard. "Well said."

I look over at her. She's smiling, a little, I think. Some teeth are showing, a couple of bottom teeth are definitely showing. I'm going ahead and counting that as a smile.

"Thanks," I mumble, clutching my Sack for the walk back up the aisle to my seat.

"Interesting," Mrs. Shepard adds.

I shrug. She never said *interesting* to Ned. Not that I care, but still.

Turn the page
to read the first part of
Olivia's story!

What Are Friends For?

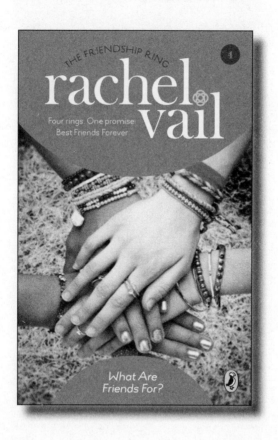

one

Some growth spurt. My mother says an inch, but I know she was tilting the book. I know it was only half an inch, maybe three quarters. She wants to reassure me, but the only time I ever think about how short I am is when everybody keeps consoling me that height doesn't matter and that anyway I'll have my growth spurt soon, when my adolescence starts.

I'm not worried about the fact that I still care about current events and my schoolwork either. I know most other seventh-grade girls have only two interests: popularity and boys. That stuff bores me, honestly; when those conversations come up—*Do you think he likes me? Are you mad at me?*—I go over my times tables in my head and wait for a more interesting topic. I know that makes me seem behind the other girls in my grade, less mature, less normal. I can't help it. It's not that I'm antisocial; I'm actually very friendly. It's just that I can't help noticing that the seventh-grade girls who used to be reasonably intelligent people have recently become idiotic, single-minded bimbos, one after another, as the hormones hit. People like CJ Hurley, a gifted ballerina and a sensitive friend, lose all perspective and every interest when some dirty-fingernailed but popular boy calls her up on the phone.

I wonder when it will happen to me.

two

This morning when I got to school, I had only a few paragraphs to go in the chapter I was reading, so I stumbled up onto the curb with the book still in front of my face. When I finished the chapter, closed my book, and looked up, Morgan Miller was staring right at me. I looked behind me to be sure it wasn't somebody else, but no, it was me.

I don't waste my time keeping up to the minute on who is in and out, but everybody in our grade knows that Morgan is always at the center of things. She tends to be very angry at somebody at least once a week and to have intense opinions about what is and isn't acceptable—clothes, behavior, all the details of life. I care a lot about moral issues like free speech and homeless people, but not so much about what an acquaintance wears. Morgan scares me a little.

So when she stared at me like that, I said something like, "You coming into school?" We've always been friendly, though distantly, and she looked particularly fierce right then. I don't care who likes me or doesn't, but it's not good to be the one Morgan is angry at.

She sprinted over to me, latched onto my arm, and dragged me by the elbow into school, whispering, "Some people think they are so great." She stormed off to her own homeroom when I asked her who.

In homeroom, permission slips for next week's seventh-grade apple-picking trip were handed out. Zoe Grandon, who sits next to me, opened her big blue eyes wide and smiled at me. I guess she was excited about the trip, which I was dreading because last year, as everybody in Boggs Middle School knows, two seventh-grade couples got caught kissing behind a haystack on the apple-picking trip. For weeks after they came back all the boys in the whole school were talking about it, pretending to cough, but really saying "hay-stacking" and meaning *kissing*. It's what made me dislike boys last year, all that talk of *hay-stacking, hay-stacking*, like all they thought girls were good for, all of us who've been their buddies and first basemen and lab partners, all they thought of when they saw us was *hay-stacking*. My brother, Dex, told me I needed to relax. He thought it was funny four of his friends got suspended. I thought the whole thing was insulting and annoying. But that's just my opinion.

All through the announcements, Zoe fiddled with a silver ring on her finger. When the bell rang and Zoe and I were walking out of the room, I complimented her on the ring.

"Thanks," she said with a huge smile. "I got it this weekend." She held her hand out for me to get a better look.

"Pretty," I said. "I like the knot."

Zoe nodded. "It's a friendship ring. CJ has the same one."

"Oh," I said. "That's nice." CJ Hurley's mother and mine are very tight; we go on family vacations together, but CJ and I aren't especially close. She is nervous and timid, and not too interested in anything but ballet, which is her life. She's very talented. Ballet and, lately, boys. And always Morgan. As far as I knew, CJ's best friend was Morgan, not Zoe.

Zoe was adjusting the ring on her finger as we got to the door of her French classroom. I decided it was none of my business who got friendship rings with whom. Zoe asked me, "Did you have fun putting together the project for English class over the weekend?"

"Fun?"

"It was harder than it seemed, I thought."

"I agree," I said. The assignment was to fill a brown paper bag with ten objects that, taken together, would give a complete picture of who you are. I'd worked all weekend on it and felt pretty confident about the ten things I'd chosen. "I can't wait to present it," I told Zoe.

CJ approached us, rubbing her right hip. I asked her if it was hurting.

She shook her head very quickly and said, "Um, a little. But, I mean, no."

"That's good," I told her as encouragingly as I could. She always seems to be in the midst of an anxiety attack.

"Thanks," she said, clasping her hands tightly behind her back. Tommy Levit walked past us. He's the boy CJ had decided she liked last week. CJ covered her face with her hands. I resisted groaning.

CJ lifted her face and announced, "Tommy asked me out."

"Oh," I said. "When?"

"Friday," CJ said.

"Congratulations." I had no more to say about that

subject. I don't know what everybody sees in Tommy Levit. He's a twin with Jonas Levit, which is inherently interesting, I guess. And he is nice-looking in a generic American way, with dimples and a sarcastic look on his face, but I really don't see why so many of the girls in our grade act stupid around him, especially after last year, when Morgan went out with him and he kissed her so hard and so unexpectedly that she dumped him and hasn't really spoken to him much since. He's the kind of boy who likes to tease— and CJ is someone who can't easily withstand teasing. But since it wasn't my business, I didn't say a thing. I opened a folder holder and put away my permission slip.

I noticed CJ watching me and realized she wouldn't be able to go, because of dance. No wonder she seemed even more tense than usual. "So you can't go on the trip, huh?" I asked her.

"What?" Zoe asked. "Why?"

Morgan, who was passing us on her way to Spanish, said, "Dance."

"Hey, wait up," CJ called to her, and chased her down the hall. She is often chasing after Morgan, apologizing or complimenting. Now Zoe chased after CJ, asking, "What is Olivia talking about, you can't go apple picking?"

CJ shook her head, trying still to catch up to Morgan. I slowed down. I hate how desperate my friends seem lately, how nervous.

"Why can't you go?" Zoe wasn't getting much response from CJ, so she turned and asked me, "Why can't CJ go apple picking?"

"We don't get back until six-thirty," I explained, since I had caught up.

"Yeah? So?"

"So," said Morgan, stopping outside Spanish. CJ almost bumped into her. "CJ has dance at four on Mondays. Not that she even likes ballet anymore, but . . ."

That surprised me. "You don't?" I asked CJ.

"It's complicated," CJ answered, nervously fingering her hair. She is so pale, you can see the veins on the side of her forehead.

"You like it or you don't," Morgan told her, with disgust in her voice. "How complicated is that?"

"You can't miss one day?" Zoe asked CJ.

CJ shook her head. "Something could happen, some casting director could come to watch. You can't. And especially, my mother?"

Morgan blew her long, dark bangs out of her eyes. "CJ's mother says, 'It's important to devote yourself to something so you'll stand out from the crowd.'"

She mimicked CJ's mother perfectly. I've heard her mother say those exact words, in fact.

"Really?" Zoe asked. "She says that?"

"All the time," Morgan answered. "Makes me feel great."

"She doesn't mean anything against you," CJ apologized. In fact, CJ's mother thinks Morgan is a bad influence on CJ, coming from a messed-up family with an immature father who ran off to California with a young floozy and a nasty angry mother with no manners. CJ's mother and mine talk every day. They both wish CJ would be best friends with me instead. CJ's hands fluttered up to her hair again. "She just, it's true that . . . I really wanted to go apple picking."

Zoe's smile tightened. "Or at least hay-stacking."

"Yuck," I said. It slipped out.

"I like apples," CJ protested in her whispery voice.

"Yeah, apples." Zoe turned the ring around on her finger. "An apple a day." The bell rang. Zoe gasped. She's the only one of us who takes French instead of Spanish. She ran back down the hall toward her class.

Morgan grabbed my elbow again and asked, "Don't you think it's pathetic when all some girls obsess about is boys, boys, boys?"

I glanced at CJ, who turned away. I didn't want to insult her, but the truth is, I do think boy-craziness is pathetic and gross. I nodded at Morgan. She yanked me into Spanish class with her.

After Spanish, Morgan pulled my arm down the corridor. The rest of me followed. Morgan whispered, "CJ thinks she's above everybody else. Doesn't she?"

I asked what she meant. CJ is a family friend; we protect each other even if we don't always enjoy each other's company.

"CJ is even more impressed with herself than usual, don't you think?"

"I hadn't noticed," I whispered back.

Morgan nodded. "Yeah, you're right. It is hard to tell, since she's always Miss Prima Ballerina. You're absolutely right."

That wasn't exactly what I had meant. I held the cafeteria door open, and Morgan dragged me through it. She walks so fast it was a challenge for me to keep up with my elbow.

"But now that Tommy Levit asked her out . . ." Morgan sighed, shaking her head. I sat down and she squeezed in beside me, at the end of the table. Morgan cupped her hand over my ear and whispered, "And did you see her ugly ring?"

"The friendship ring?" I asked.

"Yeah, hard to miss, the way they're waving their hands around, huh?" Morgan kicked off her sandals and folded her foot underneath her. "Guess CJ is pretty thrilled with herself, getting to be best friends with Zoe the Grand One."

That was witty of Morgan to come up with, I thought; nobody had ever called Zoe Grandon *the Grand One* before. I opened my 7UP and repeated, "Zoe the Grand One."

"Yeah." Morgan took one of my pretzel sticks, waved it around in a small circle beside her head, and whispered, "Hooray for them and screw us."

I laughed and the 7UP I'd just sipped went right up my nose. "Ouch," I said, which made Morgan laugh so much she had tears in her eyes. I offered her more pretzels. She was sitting so close to me I could feel the warmth from her arm on mine. I usually like more personal space than that, so I finished up lunch quickly and suggested we go outside for the rest of the period.

She said, "Absolutely"

That's another thing about Morgan—she's very emphatic. When the bell rang, she got hold of my elbow again, and we walked that way to our lockers and then to English/social studies. People watched us pass.

Every girl has her own story.
Read them all in

THE FRIENDSHIP RING series!

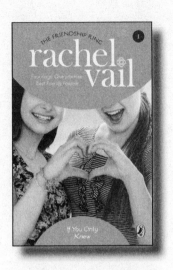

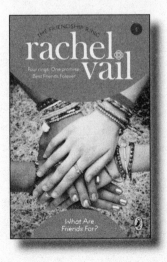

Read more from
Rachel Vail

unfriended

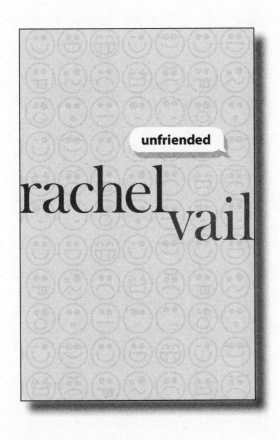